IN THE NAME OF THE FATHER
AND OTHER STORIES

IN THE NAME OF
THE FATHER

and Other Stories by

BALLA

Translated from the Slovak by

JULIA & PETER SHERWOOD

JANTAR PUBLISHING

LONDON 2017

First published in London, Great Britain, in 2017 by
Jantar Publishing Ltd
www.jantarpublishing.com

The Slovak editions of the stories in this collection were
first published in Levice by KK Bagala, L.C.A. as
'V mene otca' (2011), 'Pred rozchodom' (2005), 'Jar' (2008) and 'Nákaza' (1996).

Balla
In the Name of the Father and Other Stories
All rights reserved

Original texts © Vladimír Balla
Translation copyright © 2017 Julia & Peter Sherwood
Jacket & book design by Jack Coling

Earlier English versions of some of the stories in this collection first appeared
in the following publications: 'Before the Breakup' (Best European Fiction
2013, Dalkey Archive Press, 2012), 'Spring Is Coming' (Inventory, Princeton
University, October 2012) and 'Contagion' (Two Lines Online, March 2013).

A CIP catalogue record for this book is available from the British Library.
ISBN 978-0-9933773-5-8

Printed and bound in the Czech Republic by EUROPRINT a.s.

This book was published with financial support from SLOLIA,
Centre for Information on Literature, Bratislava.

CONTENTS

WHAT IT IS LIKE
TO READ BALLA

Reading Balla is like getting on a roller coaster and be-having in an age-appropriate manner: you never know what's coming, you scream and shout, now in fear, now in joy. Rather like the old peasant in the joke, who, taken for a joyride in a plane, imagined that anything might happen, including shitting himself, but didn't consider the possibility that the excrement might end up around his neck.

These are the kinds of corkscrew turns proffered up by Balla, to the enormous pleasure of the reader, at least if that reader happens to be me.

Let's take the following three sentences, for example:

"The river stank. This was one of the familiar scents of my youth that I loved and can summon up at will. But what would be the point?"

A perfect triple Rittberger loop. Quite wonderful. You read it, trailing after it like a rumple-headed bear on a chain.

Balla has little respect for anything, and that includes literature. You get the feeling that the only reason Balla writes is that he needs to give his liver a rest from time to time, and no serious person drinks while they're writing, though it does not necessarily follow from this that Balla is a serious person: only that, as far as we can tell, from time to time he gives his liver a rest. To read Balla is like returning to my childhood, when I invented a new sport, stream-crawling: you go along a stream, the idea being to jump from rock to rock without getting your feet wet for as long as possible, relying on divine inspiration. You jump from sentence to sentence, trying to find one that will not give way and not let you lose your balance entirely. Sooner or later you fall flat on your face.

So much for divine inspiration.

To read Balla is like being offered one of the magic sweets from Harry Potter.

Balla is the Slovak language teacher's nightmare. Now that he has been translated into Hungarian, he is the Hungarian teacher's, too.

That's why he has just one name, for the bad student has no first name: "Balla, are you deaf? Stop that at once!

I'll throw you out on your ear if you don't stop fidgeting!"

To read Balla means having no idea, when you have read him, how to answer the question: what's this book about? The original blurb claimed that "His stories take the reader into the expanses of existential intimacy, to the very depths of the anxiety that springs from loneliness."

I'd love to hear what he'd have to say about that!

In one of the stories there's a man who can't remember his past because his woman, who lives with him in a suitcase, has replaced all his internal organs with metal ones, whereupon he starts pissing screws.

That's the sort of thing he writes.

Balla's achievement in Hungarian terms is significant, in that in a number of places he vilifies Slovaks to a considerable extent. On the other hand, it's true that the Slovaks in the book are always vilifying the Hungarians. Well, you can't have everything.

GÁBOR NÉMETH
Budapest, March 2016

IN THE NAME OF
THE FATHER

"The property shall be constructed as a detached house. The windows in the basement and the bathroom facing the adjacent property shall be ventilation windows made of frosted glass. Waste will be disposed of by means of a sewage treatment system to be located a minimum of 15 metres from the well, or 30 metres in case of poor absorption"

(Planning permit No. 263/66, issued 07/02/1967 authorizing the extension and refurbishment of a family home.)

I went to see a paediatrician even though I was already twenty, and doing my military service. The nurse stressed that I shouldn't let the doctor see me in uniform; it would drive him wild as he hated soldiers, policemen, railway-men and nurses. "That's why I'm not wearing a nurse's uniform myself," the woman rattled on. So what made me go and see him anyway? Who knows, maybe I just dreamt the whole thing back in 1963, or perhaps a year earlier. To cut a long story short, I wasn't feeling well. As I walked into the surgery my eyes fell on his hands. The middle and index fingers of his right hand were missing.

"What's up?" he asked.

He examined my testicles and after feeling them for a while he made an announcement that turned out to be quite crucial later on: "Don't procreate, comrade! Don't ever procreate because you will father a predator."

I waited to hear what would come next.

The doctor went on: "However, if you marry a woman who's weak and sickly, whose teeth decay and whose hair starts to fall out by the time she's thirty, which is quite unusual in women that age, it will leave its mark on the predator you'll have fathered. The child will be born a coward. It will grow up to be someone who's a predator inside but keeps this hidden from the outside world."

He raised the index finger of his right hand by way of warning.

So he wasn't missing an index finger after all.

I sat on the cold plastic sheet covering the white examination bed with my tool hanging down and my balls in the doctor's hands. He was weighing them up.

"But maybe," he muttered, "we'll get lucky and you'll

end up impotent. Because one of them seems to be under-developed…sort of retracted…a bashful, sweet, delicate little ball." He gave my balls a yank and slapped me across the face: "No fucking, you understand?"

A reflex reaction made me kick him in the face, more of a spasm than an act of aggressive retaliation. I quickly pulled on my underpants and skedaddled. He shouted after me from the floor where he landed when I kicked him: "I know you're a soldier anyway! You think I don't have all the information on you on file? You've assaulted a doctor! You'll get locked up for this!"

As I ran away I suddenly realised I knew a woman just like that.

Exactly the sort of woman the doctor was talking about.

* * *

My son got in touch to say he wanted to sell the parental home. I still owned half of it. Actually, what really happened was that this young woman called, saying she was interested in buying the house from my son. It definitely wasn't my son who got in touch. He won't even say hello to me. It's my younger son I'm talking about. The older one isn't like that but he's moved away without even leaving an address.

I once had a father, too. He was a forester, if I remember right. He had a standard-issue horse and cart. One day he took me out with him, I can still hear the clipped sharp sound of his swishing whip. We jolted up and down as we rode along the bumpy embankment. Father made smacking noises, spitting from time to time, then suddenly pointed to a wood by the river and said: "See? I planted all that." The cart trundled off the embankment and clattered down to the edge of the forest. I jumped off into the grass and watched my father from below. He wasn't old. I've always been rather scared of getting old. And that was even before I could imagine what his old age would be like: his legs amputated little by little, the diabetes, the decrepitude. Eventually my mother had him entirely under her thumb.

There were bushes growing between the trees, some of them sick, their branches beginning to rot. Below them flickered the shiny backs of amphibians. Dampness. Father dismounted slowly and patted the horse's rear. He loved the horse more than he loved me but I'm not complaining, I don't want to take this story too seriously.

Idefigyelj, listen, my mother would say to my father in Hungarian a decade later, don't leave it all to me, you've got to make an effort, too, she said as she turned him over on his specially raised bed.

Back in the floodplains the water came up to our knees. Enormous mosquitoes were breeding in the water and swarming towards the city in huge clouds. Father reassured the neighing horse. We went deeper into the woods.

Adok én neked, just you wait, mother would say in Hungarian, panting as she turned father over.

József, she would say, reproachfully.

Idefigyelj, Ilonka, mother would begin conversations with my wife in later years, trying to attract her attention although she wasn't really keen on women, she preferred men because they listened to her, or at least they seemed to be listening, whereas women only claimed to listen. I'm listening to you, Marika, they'd say as they went on plucking a goose or raising a child, *idefigyelj*, said mother, tugging at her daughter-in-law's sleeve. She wasn't much of a listener. I'm listening to you, Marika.

Mother turned father over again.

Even people who love one another can drive each other crazy sometimes.

Father wore high rubber boots but he took my shoes off once we moved a little further away from the cart, to make sure I didn't ruin them, and left me to walk barefoot through the mud and water. My trousers were soaked through but he didn't care. I didn't make a sound even when something sharp cut into my heel, I just stopped for a moment. "Let's get a move on," he mumbled although his boots sank ever deeper. The boy needs toughening up, he used to say to his wife, my mother. He was always expecting a flood but in fact there was no flooding in Central Europe until much later, and even then our neighbourhood was never actually affected. Seeing his boots sink into the mud up to his shins I suddenly felt as if, instead of a floodplains wood, we were in the reservoir full of excrement that had been built next to the new sewage treatment plant, where the wood meets the outskirts of our town. I imagined my father sinking into the shit produced by all our neighbours. The shit generated by our entire street and all the neighbouring streets. I wished he would drown in that swamp. Was I being tough enough? He might have approved. Except that now, years later, I realise this is a false memory: by the time the sewage treatment plant was built behind Lovecká Street my father was no longer able to move.

We waded up to a mound in the middle of the wood, an island in the realm of sludge. "What was the point of trudging all the way up here?" I asked crossly, sitting on a tree stump and cradling my hurt foot in both hands. "I like it here," he snapped, lighting a hand-rolled cigarette whose smoke made my eyes sting.

My father's laziness was legendary.

He never had the slightest ambition.

Of all the people I knew in those days he was the only one who could switch off, sit down and just stay seated, puffing away without – I'm quite sure – a thought in his head. He would just sit there, immersed in emptiness. Not that he had a clue about Buddhism. His parents had come from the *puszta,* the Hungarian plain, they had a farm there. We went to visit them once, but only once, since we couldn't afford the trip again, or perhaps because my mother got into a fight with his family and that was that, once and for all. There were horses racing across the *puszta* and black pigs rolling about in the mud.

My father's parents bred grey cattle, I still remember their long horns set wide apart. And the smell of very old furniture in the long, low cottage. Its inhabitants looked like embittered bankrupt members of the middle classes driven from their bourgeois residences in Budapest by repeated blows of fate. The rooms were piled high with pungent furniture... Tiny glass cabinets crammed with religious imagery, the unnaturally cold, waxen face of the Mother of God, miniature crosses with filigree ornaments, vast quantities of goblets, glasses, tea cups, tea pots, porcelain figurines, candlesticks, knick-knacks by the thousand. Old armchairs upholstered in fabrics of various shades of purple, dark grey, dark brown, a splash of magenta on the dusty old rug. And then those outlandish ottomans... There were ottomans flanking the walls, curving to the right here and to the left there, as if made for people who had grown several heads, too many legs, countless numbers of arms. And innumerable black books, exclusively black, with greenish pages, in long rows on the bookshelves. Low ceilings, the smell of mothballs. The scent of sweet liqueurs... And silence, silence, silence everywhere, except for the floor creaking every now and then... Sturdy women in skirts, puny, wiry men in fur waistcoats, and no children, no one my age, only old people.

But why am I talking about my father?

I was fine with the relationship where I was the son and my father was the father; it doesn't really matter if it was him or someone else, basically I felt fine with the relationship where I was the son and someone else was the father. Despite all kinds of things. Despite everything. I felt quite comfortable being me in that relationship. I felt at ease in the role of a son. I was up to that role. But I don't feel comfortable with the relationship I have with my own sons. Basically, it was too early for me to be burdened with the role of a parent. Or perhaps it's my sons who are not suitable as sons. Maybe they're not the right sort of sons?

That's it: my sons don't know how to be sons.

* * *

I did want to have children.

Or did I?

In this respect I may have been different from my peers. As we grew up we gradually left our neighbourhood, but we didn't move too far away because, of course, in those days you couldn't move very far. We flew out of the nest, only to land right on an adjacent branch, so to speak. One needed an excuse, such as marriage, to justify even the shortest of flights. Although most of us were more interested in football, carpentry or plumbing, except for Barnabáš, the restless one, who had dreamt of becoming a car mechanic, but to be honest, what all of us also wanted was to have sex although, of course, we weren't too keen on its natural consequences. Or was I the only one who wasn't keen? I felt that the only thing parents could achieve through their lifelong loving care – provided they were capable of such a thing – was to alleviate the suffering they inflicted on their children by bringing them into this world. My friends may well have longed to continue their bloodline, I'd be the last person to question that. But what kind of bloodline would that be? Clans of alcoholic workers and peasants, or oafs? We're not talking the blood royal here, or some gentle, turtle-dove nation. This town's inhabitants had nothing in common with any kind of nation. Nations had dissolved in cross-border copulation while the borders kept dissolving in wars and their aftermath, constantly re-written by new generations of vagrants who drew the boundaries maliciously or blindly, waving flags and bellowing patriotic songs. They did it exactly as their ancestors and their ancestors' ancestors before them: out of habit.

* * *

It was my brother who built the house in Lovecká Street. I only gave him a hand.

We constructed a labyrinth, a maze of corridors, small rooms, dead ends and blind junctions. A substantial part of the structure was located underground, so the neighbours wouldn't be envious, while from the outside the house looked quite modest, in fact it was the smallest in the street.

Right at the outset my brother announced: "What is essential is the alternation of light and shade. Shadows will predominate. And also soft, dark corners. Curves in semidarkness. Broken arches. Modest and proletarian rather than ostentatious. Things like ribbed vaulting in the larder. All these frills are an unmistakable sign of kitsch, and that's how we'll fool everyone. The meaning will be carefully disguised."

I didn't think much of my brother's ideas.

I said nothing although I was amazed to see that instead of being straight, the floor of the corridor leading from the patio, the entrance and the hallway to the living room was at an angle, then suddenly took a leap forward, curving round in a bold sweep before reaching its destination. In the middle of the corridor a massive protrusion serving some mysterious purpose descended vertically from the ceiling, decorated with three-dimensional symbols. My brother said the symbols formed a map of the basement we were going to build. To me they looked more like Arabic script. Were we about to construct a message in Arabic in the basement? We had plenty of building materials. My brother had ordered gravel, sand, quicklime, granite blocks, lumber and steel, stressing that we would sort out the finances later, once he had negotiated a price with the suppliers. But I never got to see them. He also said that the base of the outer walls' foundation had to be at least eighty centimetres below ground level and the partition dividing the secret chambers from the living quarters would be built of solid brick.

While the house was under construction we lived in the tool shed. My brother insisted that we didn't go home but stayed there, as we also had to work at night, in fact, mainly at night. "We've got to be in tune with the building," he stressed. In the mornings, after toiling through the night, we would wash in the shed, in a white basin with rusty edges. The soap contained tiny stones, gravel and hairs. It often slipped out of our hands onto the floor soiled by our work shoes. When my brother presented his plan to me, his hands, neck and cheeks were all wet, and although he was blinking cheerfully, there was a glint of sadness deep in his eyes. "It's for you," he said, jabbing at my drenched T-shirt with his finger, "that I am building this house," he went on, poking me again, "and living in this house will provide the meaning of life, since for its residents the house itself will constitute an event more important than anything they will ever do, and that applies to whatever you do as well." He flicked his finger against my collarbone. Drops of soapy water mixed with grains of gravel and sand ran down to my navel and belt.

I can't tell if my brother really was a bricklayer.

The way he behaved.

The things he said.

The goal he pursued.

What did it all imply?

Bricklaying?

His bricklaying skills left a lot to be desired.

What was it we were building anyway?

During the day I would sleep like a log. My brother would collapse onto the sack for a few brief moments at a time. When I woke up late in the afternoons I would see only his abandoned mattress. The blankets had gone cold. He must have got up and gone to the building site hours earlier, letting me sleep on. In my absence he was occupied with activities that left no visible trace. When I joined him in the evenings, bringing neatly scrubbed hammers, bricklaying trowels, the spirit level, the triangle and compass, according to his instructions, he looked exhausted and haggard but continued working with admirable dedication. He was realising the construction and, through the construction, realising himself. I did my best, too. Naturally, we couldn't avoid making a few mistakes. For example, instead of alternating current we installed direct current in the building, as we thought it was preferable. The advantage was that I've never had to pay for electricity, which benefited the family finances considerably. Direct current can perform all the functions of normal electricity, while serving other purposes at the same time, although, absorbed as I was in the hectic pace of the construction, I never managed to ask my brother what those other purposes were. I lost contact with him in the years following the completion of the building and learned later that he had died. Meanwhile the direct current wreaked havoc. It would flash about the walls insanely, its red-hot glowing tongues lashing out uncontrollably from sockets and fuses, while at other times it would retreat and not show itself for days on end. It would just vanish without trace. Whenever that happened the lights went out and the appliances fell into a restless slumber, only to snap awake at random, without anyone turning them on.

One day my brother gave a faint smile from above the washing bowl and the flame of the candle on the window ledge made his nose, eyebrows and cheekbones flicker, alternately plunging his face into darkness and painting it again with light. I suddenly saw that he was immensely old, much older than any brother of mine could possibly have been. He declared: "The basement is vital. In fact, everything is vital. Where's my towel? No, it's definitely the basement, more than anything else. We'll have a go at it tonight. Get me a toothpick. A nail will do. I've got dirt under my fingernails."

Feeling my eyelids getting heavy I collapsed onto the inflatable bed.

My brother went off and spent the rest of the day on the building site.

When I joined him after sunset, the bulk of the work seemed to have been done. Again, I could detect no trace of activity but I didn't let this fool me. He had managed to concrete something under the floor. His face gleamed with sweat. A little love nest, it occurred to me, he's building a little love nest for me and my wife. This is how young couples imagine their first flat, their first house – as a sort of nest. Made of stalks of grass, bits of twigs, leaves. These are symbols of nature, which are, in turn, a metaphor for fertility. I don't know how I got this idea, in the cold dark basement of all places. And the other thought that flashed through my mind was that I would use the basement for storing wine, just like every good houseowner here in the south.

The centre, towards which the basement sloped steeply, was formed by the *Hwergelmir* well. The tunnels we had dug led north-eastwards, forming a symbol that spread under the workers' district. The system of corridors, the energy radiated by the algorithm beneath the roads, pavements, gardens and the suburban football pitch, was intended to bring reconciliation and indifference to the people within its range. This was how the *force* – which some people might have called sacred – was supposed to affect them, but I have my doubts: I saw my brother's drawings and the signs on the portal leading to the catacombs. The force was supposed to induce a very specific mood that would make the town's populace realise that there was no point expecting any major change and that although some day change would indeed come, for them nothing would ever change and they would remain second-rate citizens of the border region of a second-rate country. No one should try too hard, they might as well spare themselves the effort. But above all: the certainty of inevitable failure would free them from any feelings of guilt for their messed up lives.

"Initiation consists in a recurrent message stating that even initiation will be of no use to anyone," my brother explained. Perhaps he was trying to confuse me. He gave me a stern look to ensure I listened intently. "The following information will be helpful. The basement functions as a resonator. An amplifier. A transmitter! It transmits to our people the information that a state of resignation is inevitable. This is something that you need to grasp fully. You need to embrace it with all your soul."

My soul?

Did he really mean my soul?

I'm not sure I remember his words right.

Vague news of something important below the workers' neighbourhood spread by word of mouth, through conversations in pubs and on production lines; the basement was discussed at the upmarket Bastion wine bar over glasses of bitterish drink, as well as during the construction of a fence that gradually encircled the Gypsy part of town. I just listened with an embarrassed smile. I didn't understand these things back then although I could feel the pickaxe calluses on my hands and hear my brother whispering in my head: "We're doing it for their sake. All of this will make you proud one day. Forget about the odd minor imperfection in the bathroom, never mind the hastily knocked-together stairs to the attic, which will bring your wife tumbling down virtually every time. You must rise above the dysfunctional heating and drains. The essence of the house consists in something else."

And this is the house I was about to sell now, years later.

Sentiment had to be put aside. Everything had changed so much! The house had been neglected for years. After the divorce I didn't want to show my face there and my younger son had other interests, I've no idea what they were. My older son had disappeared. Nothing suggested that the building's foundations contained anything wondrous, that the foundations themselves were a wonder, that the house was possessed by some unknown force. My younger son had no idea about any of this. But as the solicitor began to put the final touches to the sales contract and the young woman who was about to become the new owner of the house started to gnaw her fingernails in a futile attempt to hide her anxiety, I could no longer contain myself and hissed to my son through gritted teeth: "You're underselling." I didn't say this because I wanted a bigger slice of the profit, far from it. It's just that I knew things about the house that he would never understand. I felt I was aware of the building's true worth even though I wasn't quite clear myself what that consisted in. But my son doesn't have a bone in his body to help him work this out. And it's all my fault! It's my educational methods that are to blame! When a friend told me recently over a cup of coffee that his daughter was out of control, that she drank, took drugs and was sleeping around, I told him: "It's your fault." He started shouting, said that everyone was blaming him but nobody would explain to him what he had done wrong.

"It's too late to ask now," I explained.

He really should have taken a different approach to raising her right from the start. I should have raised my children in a different way, too. I should have followed the example of, say, my neighbour Római, whose son loved him because he could find no rational explanation for the cruel and patronizing nature of an older man, for his father's coldness. On the other hand, his son was in awe of the impenetrable male world, and had learned not only to fear his father but also to admire him. And he also trusted him, for he knew that his father would always protect him and keep him on the straight and narrow. Római taught his son that membership of the communist party was an instrument to be used cunningly for the family's benefit. He himself had held a minor position on the town party committee and even carried a gun in his briefcase, believing someone might want to eliminate him. This was complete nonsense, of course: nobody in our small town would raise a finger against a communist. People had succumbed to total apathy. They felt indifferent even towards bastards of the highest order. All they did was sit back and twiddle their thumbs in unison, waiting for someone to come along and liberate them from the communists.

I remember our last night at the building site. With an expansive gesture my brother swept all the junk off the table in the toolshed and said, spreading out on the table top a pile of books he had produced from a sack: "Here you are, read. You've got to read because you are stupid and blind and don't know how to interpret the signs."

* * *

In later years I devoted a lot of time to books.

I read about the importance of silence and I realised that the closest I personally had ever got to it was not talking to my family. In the silence, a gentle rustling, a kind of dry whispering sound could be heard: it was me lying on the couch picking my nose. In those days I didn't think it was disgusting.

I wasn't aware of being observed.

But my younger son had been observing me. And that is one of the reasons he began to hate me.

Mind you, he would have ended up hating anyone if he had observed them for long enough.

* * *

We're moving into the house in Lovecká Street.

I'm carrying a bag with our lunch and the documents in one hand and a rocking horse in the other. The rocking horse is my older son's favourite toy. The younger one hasn't been born yet, he's not even a twinkle in his father's eye. My wife is walking ahead of me. She opens the door, enters and lets go of the door, which slams shut abruptly, hitting the head of my son's wooden toy.

The glass in the door shatters, spilling onto the pavement.

The patio where we are standing in silence affords a view of a large empty field. Later, especially in the winter, we would often see hares and deer there, sometimes even the odd furry creature. At the end of the field there are woods and a little further on is the sewage plant. The sun is setting behind the plant's dark blue dome covered in metal sheeting. A dirt path leads from the house to the field. Around it there is room for planting a garden.

"This is where we'll put up some pens and a chicken coop," my wife says.

I don't say anything, trying to imagine a football pitch. My son must become a football player. That's what real men are like: they have bodies made to pick up girls but also to make money. That's what it's all about.

"We'll play football behind the garden."

"In the field?"

"I'll fence off a bit and put up some goalposts."

Now that's what a good father sounds like! I'm proud of myself but I feel self-conscious at the same time. Will I be up to it? Will I rise to this challenge? My own house, my own wife, a child. Responsibilities. Neighbours – they're strangers and who knows if they'll accept us. Just as well the house is small and inconspicuous. It won't make them envious. On the other hand, they'll laugh at us behind our backs. Our neighbours have big mansions, or at least bigger, wider plots of land, with chickens running to and fro, it's almost like the countryside. After all, Lovecká is the last street in town. The outskirts. We can look forward to tranquillity, quiet evenings, in the summer we'll grill greasy bacon on a bonfire under the fruit trees.

I look over to the left, into the yard next door.

A tall bony man is struggling to throw a huge rug onto a metal contraption. His wife comes out of the house, greets us in Hungarian and walks down the stairs. She picks up a rug beater and soon we hear sounds of swishing and pounding. The poultry in the courtyard stay put, the chickens don't even squawk. They're used to it. We might get used to it too, I think to myself, picking up the rocking horse. But at the same time I'm beginning to dread the impending numbing torpor, because that's what usually breeds a routine.

I look at the shards of glass gleaming on the pavement. The next day I replace the damaged door.

* * *

After I was demobbed I got a job as a storeman in a hardware shop. I started under the supervision of older colleagues, men in their forties, whom I respected. Much later, when I was in my forties myself, I realised they didn't deserve my respect. A forty-year-old is a kid, maybe a bit older and less agile, but still a kid, a disillusioned, irritable and vindictive kid. What's rational about that? Will rationality come with age? I've been waiting for it for years. Jesus, those neurotic, frustrated, middle-aged kids! Full of unsatisfied yearnings and fearful of never being able to satisfy them. A forty-year-old is significantly worse off than an inexperienced naïve youngster, since he's aware of the time he has wasted, is unstable and tends to acts rashly.

But back then I knew nothing about that.

What really mattered to me was football. Our town stadium, though quite large, would be packed whenever we played. Early in the morning I used to go out for a run on the river embankment in a tracksuit full of holes, come winter or summer, rain or shine, mud or dust. Hungry, without breakfast. That's the best way to run. On the embankment I sometimes hallucinated out of hunger and exhaustion. That was a sign it was time to stop and take a break. Whenever that happened I felt like a failure. I would sit in the grass for a while, arms akimbo, taking deep breaths and looking at the river. The dirty water flowed slowly as if intent on coming to a halt. Its surface was covered in yellow-brown foam. And fish, floating belly up. Small children would poke at them with sticks. After hauling out a few cadavers they would feed the toxic meat to the feral cats. Then they would toss the cats' bodies, writhing in their death throes, into the water. It looked as if the river was populated not just by fish but also by cats, killed by the foam from the Šurany sugar refinery, just like the fish. The river stank. This was one of the intimate scents of my youth, one that I love and can summon up at will. But what would be the point? I used to sit in the grass, gathering strength to go on running. Or I would get up and keep on running to gain more strength. It's making the effort that generates the strength for more effort. That's what sport is all about. That was something I understood well. Torture yourself so you can better endure more torture. These days it strikes me as slightly weird. I have some friends of my sons' age, who go running, lift weights, sweat, pant. Children! They dream of the future. In a nutshell: forty-year-olds. My friend Gál is like that. He walks erect like a candlestick, for want of a more original comparison. Or maybe: erect like a cock? Pardon my language. He's a textbook example of someone who has not given up hope that he might still get younger and go back to his childhood, if only he exercised religiously, subjecting himself to some painful regimen. Then he'll start a new life. He'll avoid those mistakes. This time round he won't become a waiter. From a tender age he will focus on programming, on computer applications. Except where will all those computers have gone by the time he grows up again? Will he still be able to get away with ripping off people buying computer parts? Will computer piracy still exist? What will replace it Gál has no idea. He doesn't know what exactly he ought to do in this new childhood of his, what goals to pursue to ensure he's not caught unawares by his next fortieth birthday. My younger son may also have taken up sport. Although the last time I saw him in the solicitor's office it didn't seem that way. A round belly, sallow complexion, droopy shoulders, scrawny legs, a listless expression. I guess he's a beer drinker. A beer philosopher. He'd do better to follow Gál's example. But it might all amount to the same thing: my younger son is not getting any younger either. To say nothing of me. Although I still feel fine.

I'd been working at the warehouse for about three months when a new girl was hired to work at the counter. She was clever. She had a nice voice. When she was on the phone, customers at the other end of the line must have imagined a beautiful young woman. Beautiful she wasn't. But she wasn't ugly either. Average? Good enough for me. A young sportsman needs sex. That's a big truth. But the girl was above-average pretty. A few days later I discovered she wasn't a girl but a mature woman, five years my senior. I should have realised the looming danger straight away. Except what could I have realised at that age? A twenty-year-old with a crew cut? I lived a simple bachelor's life in those days: running along the embankment in the morning was followed by work at the warehouse and cracking jokes with my colleagues, then a workout, a game of football, tiredness, the night, followed in turn by another morning, have I left anything out? Oh yes, my sexual fantasies. Fantasies featuring non-existent women, assembled from fragments of existing ones. My ideal woman was made up of the legs of one woman, the hips of another, the breasts of a third, the smell, voice, and movements of yet other women. She was invariably a woman without a soul, personality or preferences, who responded obediently to my every demand, letting me turn her over without protest and who didn't giggle if I happened to come prematurely. But what did I know then about what prematurely means?

I wasn't aware of the looming danger.

I wasn't aware of the trap to which I was drawn like a mouse intoxicated by cheese.

Like a cat intoxicated by a mouse.

* * *

I don't see why I should give anyone preferential treatment, just because that person happens to be my son. All right, I wouldn't kill him. But that's about it. He's just a stranger to me. I don't give a fuck about sentiment, not a bloody fuck. I haven't seen my sons for years, we haven't talked for years, everything that once was has now vanished, evaporated, gone. They might look like me for all I know, but so what? I'm sure I resemble lots of people! I'm an ordinary, forgettable man. The type that gets forgotten. A friend once told me I reminded him of a Pink Floyd guitarist. So? When the guitar player dies I won't shed a tear. And when I die the guitar player won't shed any tears either. Although he might find out that I had died, everything is on the net these days. The net is *pontifex,* the bridge builder, like the pope. Why shouldn't

I kill my sons? Just to ensure the survival of my genes? I couldn't care less about my genes. Abraham didn't hesitate to raise his knife to Isaac. All right, he had a mission. He thought it was God's command. God is quite an authority for some people. By the way, I think Abraham was off his head. Did nobody notice the knife-wielding old man was going round the bend? But perhaps it's me who's going round the bend, and that's why I don't communicate with God. It's quite enough that my wife used to. In any case, I admit that bringing Abraham into this doesn't really support my case. But anyway: what do I care about my sons now? Parents are automatically expected to consider their lives complete once they've brought children into this world. After that they're supposed to live for them, to focus exclusively on shaping their existence. Am I supposed to be ashamed just because I keep pursuing my own, personal happiness? And my joy? Regardless of what sort of life the runts have built for themselves? Am I supposed to be ashamed that I'm still doing fine as a man, as a partner? Or am I meant to be living just for their sake? They're alive, I've moved on, and I'm alive too. I might be living on my pension but I'm alive. In the history of this continent there have been times when parents didn't pamper their children: they had so many of them they had no reason to pamper them. A child would get hurt and die, another was damaged from the start, a third might be sold and a fourth mislaid somewhere. Let's say those weren't the best of times. But the fact is, people did live that way, too. Call me old-fashioned, even medieval in this respect. I understand that my younger son doesn't love me. I've never given him any reason to love me. And even if I had, it was a long time ago. Perhaps his memory doesn't serve him well. Has he forgotten the kite I made for him? He broke it in the door leading to the garden where the chicken coop was. The kite never got a chance to take off. After all the trouble I went to with that piece of junk! Admittedly, one kite isn't much for an entire childhood. But perhaps there were other kites. How many kites did the whippersnapper really break? He has no right to expect emotion and love from his father, it's not something he can take for granted.

Compulsory love?

Compulsory concern?

I'm not cut out for that.

* * *

The first time I laid eyes on Ľalika in Lovecká Street I found the sight of her so revolting it made me retch. She had moved next door with her husband and daughters a year after us. I thought her beak of a nose particularly repulsive, but her enormous rear in those blue tracksuit bottoms was revolting too. That the idea of adultery with this unattractive, obviously stupid and malicious female could have crossed my mind at that point is simply out of the question.

* * *

The era of the great blackout began with the drawing of the drapes across our kitchen window. My wife announced in the semi-darkness that the window would stay covered so that people outside wouldn't see what we were up to. She claimed the neighbours could see into our kitchen. She ascribed fundamental importance to this. She got it into her head that our neighbours' sole purpose in life was to spy on our family: on intimate scenes as well as everyday dining in the kitchen. Our neighbours were also able to see into our bathroom and could therefore watch a parade of naked bodies. That's what they're after, my wife sobbed, and that's what you're after too!

She was beginning to lose the plot.

I'm saying this because that's exactly what happened.

Idefigyelj, Ilonka, my mother said to my wife in Hungarian a few days later, when she came to visit us, why have you drawn the drapes? It's pitch dark in here. I can't even see my coffee. She felt her way around the kitchen tablecloth until her fingers knocked into the cup of coffee. Oh dear, I hope I won't make a big mess here, she said, promptly making a big mess. *Bocsánat*, it's only because it's so dark here, she apologized without really meaning it. Her tiny frame, tinier with each passing year, was shaken by a giggle I remembered from my childhood. My mum's siblings, my uncles and aunts, used to say she was a malicious dwarf. That's harsh. But can anyone honestly claim there aren't any malicious dwarfs in this world?

One day a schoolmate of my younger son came to see us. He was a fit, jolly, cheeky, healthy boy. Now that's what I'd call a son! Sitting with my younger one in the dark kitchen the handsome bright boy suddenly blurted out: "What's going on here, you having a blackout?"

That's exactly what it was: a blackout.

My younger one was embarrassed and said nothing.

I walked past wearing my usual serious frown and greasy overalls. I didn't find the overalls smelly, I actually liked the smell of oil, of the oil growth rings, the sediment of years gone by. There were some screws and nails rattling in my pocket, just in case I suddenly felt like tightening something or screwing something on, and as I was passing the kitchen on my way to the bathroom to get some swarfega I slowed down a bit, curious to hear what my younger son would reply to his classmate.

But the little nincompoop said nothing.

I'm being unfair, I know. I understand his silence, his shame. How was he to explain to his classmate that his mum was in a sulk? Because at first that's what it looked like, and only gradually did her behaviour become clearly pathological.

What was I to do, how was I to help my son?

I made myself scarce as fast as I could.

* * *

When I walked home from work in winter my hair and clothes would often get drenched by snow. There wasn't much warmth at home either, and the tense atmosphere would soon drive me out into the garage. I would sit on a rickety chair at my desk shivering. A ginger tomcat made its home in the garage. The whole place hummed as the cat purred. Otherwise silence reigned, and there was just me, the silence, the tomcat, the old Škoda, and the pit where we stored potatoes and apples. I'd never known such moments of solitude as a child or a young man. Is it strange that I'd never known these things until I got married? Is it unusual? I certainly thought so at the time.

Every now and then the tom would set off for a silent walk along the top shelves of the tool cabinets, leaping from one to the next and keeping his eyes on me. I don't believe that cats carry unfathomable worlds hidden in their heads. I used to regard the tomcat as a mysterious being. This is how faith in something higher expresses itself: in the idea of a profound meaning hidden behind the green eyes of a cat, its pupils dilating and then narrowing again, as if the animal were transmitting signals. It's God's Morse code, the narrow and dilated pupils standing for dots and dashes, I would ruminate in the garage, deciphering the feline transmission, with my head wet and brain swollen, I'm dead serious.

And I thought about escaping.

But where could I escape to? My mother? I had never loved her as a child and I wasn't sure I could stand living with her. It's only in childhood that you cling to a mother, even though some varieties of motherhood can be really rough.

Gradually I adapted the garage to provide longer-term shelter but that could hardly have been regarded as an escape. It led out into the same yard. In the evenings I would look out from the garage into the same windows of our neighbours' house. Only the angle was different. And I pondered where my love for my wife had gone. Was I capable of love? Or: had I been capable of it in the past? Because even that could have changed over time. I wandered about the place, skirting around boxes, piles of spare V-belts, I've no idea what I needed so many belts for, to cover piles of other things, as sometimes I would camouflage unnecessary stuff with other unnecessary stuff, out of laziness maybe? I would stop at the window in the evening and stare into the cold wintry yard. The world was bathed in a cold light. The tom narrowed its eyes languidly. Is it possible that what I had once felt wasn't love but pride? Pride at the fact that I, too, had succeeded in attracting a woman and becoming her one and only? That I was able to fulfil a woman's life in terms of her need for a husband? What made this a real achievement was that this woman was older and more experienced. But not too old! That would have devalued the achievement. Also intellectually I was her equal even though she had a five-year head start in terms of experience. I know that my younger son, when he grew up, also had a relationship with an older woman. But she must have been particularly sensible because she got rid of my younger son in time, thus saving him. She saved him having to agonise over her faded beauty, inventing morally sounder, decent, acceptable and forgivable reasons for breaking up beyond the simple fact that his beloved had grown old and no longer attracted him, that she was no longer attractive to anyone, that you could no longer, what I'm trying to say is that you could no longer – you know what I mean – that's right. Well, it's not that you couldn't. You could always, why not? But things get fatal when you can no longer boast about your wife and about having sex with her and when, in fact, you'd rather pretend that you don't even know her. The process of ageing, fading, the connection between a wilting body and wilting feelings – we might be duplicitous and keep quiet about it but if we do raise the subject, we tend to cover up the essence with hollow chatter about burnout and alienation. Along the lines of: we've grown apart, we no longer understand one another. Alienation? When were you close to the old hag, I ask? Never. Because when you were close, she wasn't like this, she didn't look like this! Closeness...closeness... Not even habit helps because the minute you finally get used to something being bad things get even worse, and they get worse with every passing day. That's how ageing works. And now add obesity to the equation. Or emaciation, as the case may be. Skinny dry calves instead of full ones. My younger son was lucky to have met a sensible woman.

She saved him. I wasn't so lucky. I know, it's heartless to talk like that, but the difference between me and most men is that I'm heartless and say so while others are heartless but don't let on, even though they think and see things the way I do. They claim to have got used to their partners, asserting they could no longer live without them. But living with them the way they do when they can't live without them is not the life they had dreamt of when they embarked on this project. And I wanted to behave responsibly in marriage. But how can a young man in the early days possibly imagine how it will all end? You can't suppress the male in the male. If you do, there are consequences. You'd have to suppress your natural instincts. I'm not trying to sound like a champion of natural instincts, and I don't mean those cases where these instincts are exceptionally powerful either. So how does it all end? It all starts with desires that are, of course, satisfied by the wife. Two or three times a day. Later, even if the wife is willing – and she's not – later something is missing. And it's at Christmas that everything that isn't working smoothly comes to a head. I have spent many a Christmas in the garage. Invariably it would start in the morning as we were decorating the Christmas tree. The first problem was that my wife wanted a pine tree rather than a spruce. All our neighbours had managed to get hold of pine trees, no idea where they had picked them up. Obviously, they must have started planning their family Christmas back in October. But I had other things on my mind in October. Like musing about the thighs of my female colleagues, the shop assistants, those thighs under their blue lab coats, those thighs that were awake, still smelling of summer or at least of September, still lightly tanned and soaked in sun.

What is Christmas for?

It's for catalyzing a family crisis.

It's for highlighting all the problems in a relationship.

It's for abusing the husband, the wife and the children.

That's the idea. And who came up with this idea? Families where everything works perfectly well. The one thing they're missing is being the object of the intense envy of other families that are dysfunctional. We're happy, our relationships work but at the same time we sympathize with those who aren't so lucky. We desperately need those unlucky ones so that we can feel sorry for them. And if there are no such families around, we'll create them. We'll drum into them how unhappy they are! Because other-wise – who would we have to needle with our happiness?

That's what Christmas is for.

* * *

I heard noises coming from the basement.

Down there, in the semi-darkness, I found my wife pounding the concrete floor with a pickaxe. Sparks were flying, the concrete was cracking. She didn't see me but she must have smelled my greasy overalls.

A long crack ran across the floor.

I didn't know what to say.

I said: "Digging, are you?"

"I'm liberating."

"What are you liberating?"

"Whatever it is you've imprisoned there. You and your brother. It's down there."

"What?"

"The seed. It would have sprouted long time ago if it weren't for this damned…thick…horrible…concrete…"

My wife was panting as she swung the pickaxe. "You and your brother! Did you do it on purpose? You've buried it. Did you think it would stay buried forever? Get out of here. You're tormenting me. You're burning me up!"

Something was burning her up?

"I've had enough of your lies!" she screamed.

I looked around: "My lies? I didn't say anything. I'm silent. We never talk. You're impossible to talk to."

"I can feel every single word you're holding back. You make me sick!"

I made myself scarce as fast as I could.

* * *

Valerian had started to grow by the steps below the patio. Cats would rub against it blissfully until they reached a state of ecstasy. My sons, after consuming it, would soon go to sleep, their heartbeat slowed down. The herb helped the boys cope with the tension that reigned in the house. Their mother served them the magic brew every night instead of tea. The older one didn't grumble, he was already broken. The younger one didn't notice anything. After dinner they would run out into the wood behind the garden and clamber up the trees in a languid, somnolent way, falling off and climbing up again but never bawling, they were too shy for that, too downtrodden by the atmosphere in the house with its daily spectacle of their equally downtrodden parents. Their mother was genuinely downtrodden and I pretended to be downtrodden too. I didn't want to antagonize anyone with my joy. The joy that would grip me every time I thought of my female colleagues. I felt young. But I never showed any of my joy and youthful exuberance at home. Lounging in front of the television I would reflect on what goes on between fathers, mothers and children. I avoided the marital bed since nothing ever happened there anyway. I usually drifted off in the middle of my couch reflections but before falling asleep I managed to figure out the odd thing or two and it was making me more and more unhappy. My marriage was a wreck. This fact disfigured my face like a boil, putting my unhappiness on public display: my face grew ashen and acquired a disdainful expression. I gritted my teeth and clenched my jaws. My teeth are still in great shape although I'm a stranger to toothbrushes. The muscles beneath my skin throbbed. My neighbours disguised such subtleties, never airing the secrets of their family hearth in public even though they had plenty of filthy linen to wash. My neighbour, Római, had a daughter as well as a son. He often punched her so hard it would send her flying several yards, but he did so in the privacy of his own home. That's how disputes were resolved in their house. His son, a friend of my younger one, told me about it. But in fact, Római isn't a good example when it comes to covering up family problems. He had no qualms about dealing with intimate problems out in the street: he would chase his son with an axe all the way down Lovecká Street and into the woods where, fortunately, the boy always managed to disappear among the trees.

I've never threatened my sons with an axe.

Maybe that's what gave the impression that I didn't care about them.

* * *

My wife and I never went out together, except once a week to church. She walked by my side embarrassed to be seen with me. She thought everyone in town was aware of my adultery. She felt deeply humiliated.

I knew how she felt.

"Can I buy you a cup of coffee?" asked the priest one day, coming up to us after mass. My wife froze. She didn't know what to do. There was a café not far from the church. We went in. My wife had never been there before but she noticed that the priest knew his way around. Not as much as I did. This was a place I often brought my female colleagues in the evenings. This was where I spun my webs around them. I could be very eloquent and entertaining at times like that. Unlike at home. At home it was as if everything inside me was blocked. But what was the point of being witty at home? At home my wit would have been wasted.

Straight away, a cup of coffee and a glass of mineral water materialised in front of the priest.

"I know what's been going on in your house," he said, leaning over to my wife the minute we sat down. My wife shot me a horrified look. I stirred my hot drink wordlessly. I was on edge. The priest hadn't picked the best way to start. That's not what we'd agreed! I had hoped he would be more discreet and take a more roundabout route. My wife would then open up to him of her own accord. But it really was my mistake, I hadn't realised how he wanted to play it: his invitation was meant for my wife alone. How could she open up to him with me, the source of her unhappiness, sitting right there? I was the one she blamed for all her unhappiness, because she took me far too seriously. If she had ignored me everything could have been fine.

Sheepishly I inspected the familiar fittings of the café, the chair covers, the coffee machine. Stemmed glasses were stacked in rows above the bar like in a glass factory.

"You are an exceptional woman," the priest said.

"Exceptional? Why? People generally think I'm strange, but not exceptional. What's that supposed to mean? Are you behind all this?" my wife exclaimed turning to me abruptly, even though, when we had first met, she wasn't prone to abrupt gestures. But as the years went by she gradually lost her dignity and self-control. She would even assault me physically, flailing her arms about and prancing around so that I would have to get hold of her and pin her down.

I glanced at the priest and replied with a shrug: "Just wanted to help. Something's got to be done. You ought to talk to someone. So I was thinking...."

"You and your wife are in the same boat," the priest chipped in. "The Lord is above us but we both sense that this is not quite enough, because we are here and He is so very far away."

My wife went pale. "You are a priest, an educated man. And yet you pretend we are equals in matters of faith?"

Instinctively she lowered her voice so I wouldn't hear.

I got up and walked over to the window and looked out into the street. There were many pretty girls passing by. And although I still could hear the priest and my wife, by leaving the table I signalled that they could talk freely. I knew I couldn't leave altogether, I was sure my wife would run after me. At least I thought she would. She wasn't used to strangers.

I simply had to try and do something, as the situation in the basement was getting out of hand. I hoped my wife would find renewed comfort in the watered-down religion offered by the church. I wanted this to be over with, I wanted to make sure that spirituality would not reach our basement, stop this barbarous thing growing out of the cracked concrete, this was insane, none of the men in our street had ever mentioned anything like that. Having a prayer book is one thing but to have *Yggdrasil* growing in one's basement is quite another. My wife offered contradictory information on the subject. At first she claimed it was my brother who had planted the tree, only to set it in concrete under the floor later. That didn't make sense to me even though there were many things I wouldn't have put past my brother. My wife assured me that down in the basement, below the concrete, the ancient Nordic sacred tree was getting ready for the big day when it would burst through the barrier. For the time being it was gathering strength in the inert, rigid, cold world down below. It had no need of sunlight. The sun was the last thing it needed! Still, my wife was becoming impatient and wanted to free the plant from under the concrete with a pickaxe. Later, after we'd had a few fistfights down in the basement, she admitted she was the one who had planted the tree, by mistake. What she had wanted to plant was the tree of knowledge. They had sold her the wrong kind of seed at the garden centre. She even showed me the packet with a few remaining seeds and its red and yellow lettering. I had always assumed trees were all more or less the same but our clashes over the Christmas tree made the scales fall from my eyes. My wife wanted to reach God by climbing this tree, that was her idea, but the question is, what kind of God would she have reached? And was there really a God waiting up there in the celestial heights? Has the expansion of Christianity left any room for a God? The traffic in our basement certainly ended up being exclusively one way, downwards, with the spirits of evil, disruption and unrest descending upon us. So I preferred to put my wife in touch with the priest, as the path to heaven he was offering seemed harmless to me. The priest was sure to find a solution, I thought. By the way, isn't it commendable that I survived a few more years of marriage in such circumstances? Although I should also bear in mind what those years meant for my family. In short, some people seem to be incapable of living their lives. Admittedly, we've had some nice moments, too. Maybe for my sons these were the moments they spent in the company of their friends, who knows. And for my wife? She was fine when I was at work and she was home alone with the kids. Those were her best moments: in addition to the usual fables and fairy tales she would feed them all sorts of unsavoury information about me. The children gradually fell for these rumours and lies and began to treat them as facts. Yet there are plenty of mothers who, in order to give their offspring a well-adjusted upbringing, tend rather to burnish the image of their father so that they have someone to look up to. Which makes the children more resilient and gives them a positive role model so that they face the future with faith in marriage and traditional values. My wife inculcated my children with false information about my genetically inferior character. She claimed that people whose eyebrows meet in the middle are horrible and heartless. Where did she get that idea from? If she had known it all along, why did she marry me in the first place? Was she attracted to evil?

It was no use crying over spilt milk.

"You're right, I'm confessing to you!" said the priest, smiling at her. He leaned back in his seat and crossed his legs. Then, with a grave expression, he leaned towards her: "Let's say a prayer together, shall we? In the name of the Father and the Son and the Holy Spirit…. Oh, and there's one point I want to stress: you and I know exactly what we mean by this prayer of ours. We know that from time to time you have to make a sacrifice for the sake of our Lord. By doing something you find unpleasant."

"But it's not that I find my husband unpleasant, I find him downright repulsive. All that sweating and straining of his. And his foul breath!"

"Everyone has foul breath. You too, sister. I bet you've got problems with your teeth."

"That runs in my family."

"So, basically, it's a matter of God's will. I understand."

"Exactly. But my husband doesn't even brush his teeth. He never takes a bath either. He only goes to the bathroom to ogle our neighbours' naked wives."

"We've been through this already, sister. Come now, that's quite innocent! These days you don't commit a sin just by looking. Or rather, you do but it's not taken seriously anymore. I wish that was the worst thing that ever happened!" The priest gave a hearty laugh. "Besides, if you continue to reject your husband as a man, you mustn't be surprised… Because marital duties are like those in a monastic order, they're most sacred when we don't really feel like fulfilling them, even it's for understandable reasons."

"But I've already told you…"

"That's it, exactly. And that's what makes the family hearth die out. That's what breeds conflict and, eventually, truly sinful thoughts. Morality is under threat if a man who is bound to his one and only helpmeet is prevented from satisfying his natural desires. Because his wife is not willing. Because she resists. She fights him in bed. She whispers words of refusal, insults even. And the children get to hear everything. Can you see, sister, how you've damaged your marriage? Or indeed, marriage as a whole, as an institution! But now, let's have a chat about the tree."

"About…the tree?"

"Yes, the tree you've been experimenting with in the basement, like Michurin, the Russian botanist!" thundered the priest, bringing his fist down on the table.

* * *

On occasion I tried to have a conversation with my younger son but it usually ended in an uneasy silence. I blame intergenerational conflict, although lack of practice also had something to do with it. Besides, I was absent-minded, unable to elaborate on any subject since what was on my mind was not a topic fit for discussion with a son. I wanted someone to whom I could boast of my relationships, of my conquests, but my son was hardly the right audience for this kind of talk and neither were my neighbours. They wouldn't have understood me at all. They lived for their families and this showed in their appearance. Boorish, badly groomed, overweight, the only thing they dreamt about was money, it's no different today. It had never crossed my mind to tell my son how I met his mother, even though it's a nice story, a nice romance, as were my subsequent affairs with female colleagues. It began the same way, with smiles and glances, only back then I was barely twenty, and while running errands between the warehouse and the shop with its tasteful display of wares – nowadays they would pass neither for wares, nor for a tasteful display – I started noticing this young woman, in the mid-sixties this was, the young woman looked very attractive in her lab coat: she had hair, breasts, legs, in short, all the feminine attributes. I was driven by lust and my body performed to perfection.

Was I supposed to tell my son that I find women attractive?

Tell him about the conversations, the flirting, the excitement, the restlessness of an alpha male?

As I could hardly wait till the following morning to see out how an affair might develop, I would usually fall silent in my son's presence and quickly get on with making improvements to the garage. At that time it was just a kind of wooden shed. My younger son would sometimes follow me there, he was probably bored indoors. Or was it because he wanted to stay close to me at all costs? His friends were at least able to tag along with their fathers to the pub and watch them bellowing and downing drinks and that would have made them feel like grown men. My son didn't get that chance because I wasn't interested in pubs. The seedy boozing monsters repelled me. The repugnant mugs, the mouths full of chipped, blackened teeth, the chapped lips, the cauliflower noses with purple pimples sent out a clear message: it's too late for us to get under young salesgirls' skirts. This was something I was constantly aware of. Why would I go to a pub? I wouldn't even touch a small beer after lunch. However, I did collect beer bottle caps, which came in handy as underlay for attaching tarpaper to the wooden frame of the garage. My younger son would pass me the caps and short nails and together we would repeat the mantra "nail – cork", even though, as far as I know, a bottle cap is not a cork. It's a nice memory anyhow. The memory of the mantra. But eventually the whole garage was covered with tarpaper and that was the end of my cooperation with my younger son.

At the shop it was Drdavá, the cashier, that I got on with best. It's a shame she had to waste a lot of precious time with customers who came by the shop even though there was virtually nothing to buy there. Sometimes the odd bike would turn up, or a highly defective hair drier, a mesh roll, a wire bundle, a bunch of nails and screws, but those I preferred to take home. So what? My neighbour Peterič was a clerk at the Váhostav building company and he brought home enough material from work for a loft conversion, plus he constructed a neo-gothic gazebo in the back of his garden. That's where he would sit watching my wife's legs as she did the gardening. But before long her legs had gone fat, her thighs flabby. I have always been a very critical observer of these matters. Peterič, too, had gradually gone all flabby. He's pushing up the daisies now. Our son, brother, husband, father, grandfather has left us, his death notice said. Those were the positions he held. I'll never be a grandfather. My sons have deliberately deprived me of the joy of having grandchildren. Or rather, is the fact that they don't have children their personal tragedy?

I ought to let them in on the secret that children are not necessarily a blessing.

When I spilled the beans to Drdavá about my wife's exploits in the basement, she said a lot of women did things like that. That really surprised me. If only I knew what was going on in the basements of our town! Drdavá had a rigorously logical way of thinking, unencumbered by mystical tendencies, nevertheless she sometimes dabbled in occult practices, in a purely pragmatic sort of way: only when the need arose to put a spell on someone or to influence the turn of events. She proposed that we resort to a well-known occult practice, whereby a serious interpersonal issue is transformed and summoned up in the shape of an ethereal being, which is subsequently annihilated by being uncoupled from its spiritual source.

One day, in an attempt to save my marriage, Drdavá and I created a biomorphic monster in the warehouse. It's hard to describe what it looked like. First a puddle of slime formed on the floor. The process also produced an aural effect, a slurping...a kind of slurping...how should I put it? It was more than just a sound. Words fail me. Suddenly there was this strange smell and then we saw the monster. But my marriage fell apart anyway because the creature we summoned up survived, and so the ritual failed. This is also reflected in the general state of relationships today.

* * *

The house in Fatranská Street where I grew up wasn't really a house, just a makeshift room in some sort of a shed. There wasn't a single book in the room except for a slim volume of Hungarian folk recipes but even that lay untouched on top of the wooden cabinet of a radio that was permanently tuned to the same station. My mother cooked by instinct. Always the same dish. I'm not resentful, just stating a fact. Should I claim that we lived in a villa when we actually lived in a shed? Should I claim she was a great cook when in fact I was brought up on bean soup? The radio speaker was covered by a piece of sackcloth. I pinned my collection of military stars and badges on it. In front of the radio stood a bowl in a metal stand. When we still lived with my parents, this was where my wife used to wash her breasts. Gleaming white, they reminded me of throbbing creatures with a life of their own. My father would lie motionless on the sofa covered by eiderdowns, his head turned towards the centre of the room. He watched the half-naked young woman while diabetes was busily working away at his toes. I wonder if his parents had prepared him to cope with this sort of illness while he was growing up. I doubt it. Parents are more likely to inculcate their children with useless things. They don't tell you any of the crucial stuff, not out of malice but to cast a spell on the future: what we don't speak of won't happen.

My wife washed her breasts and blushed.

That's when she began to hate my father.

When she began to hate me, I don't know.

My father never left the room, he just lay there without sleeping, though the fact that he wasn't asleep didn't necessarily mean he was awake. His eyes stayed open, my wife never forgot that. She kept reminding me of that, yelling that I was a whoremonger, just like my father. "He wanted me, a thousand times over he wanted to have me!" she yelled.

She was unable to really understand the peculiar, unwakeful manner of his wakefulness.

There really were no books in our household, such was the world of Fatranská Street we grew up in, we, the bookless descendants of our uneducated bookless ancestors. That was another reason the state could treat us any way it liked. And it's also why the state never amounted to anything much. And although nowadays I have lots of books, I still can't resolve my relationship with my sons. I'm pretty sure that they, too, have lots of books, yet they don't know what to do about their relationship with me. Perhaps this failure to resolve things is their way of resolving things. Or perhaps they don't in fact see our relationship as a problem and have written me off already.

Who was the first to start this writing off business?

* * *

My younger son once asked me to make him a kite. Yes, well, there had been times when he tried to engage with me. But it happened rarely. My older son had no time for me either. He preferred to withdraw into silence, eventually disappearing altogether, and I no longer see him around town, which is not something I can say about my younger son. Just the other day I saw him walking down the street with a pretty woman. They both looked at me without a trace of emotion. I realised that the woman knew me. My younger son must have told her about me. Oh great, thanks very much! We ran into each other near the former Soviet military base that we used to call *Russian* though most of its inhabitants were fierce-looking Asians. I had numerous opportunities to confirm this, as on my way to work I would come across troops out on their morning exercises. Russians, I would say to myself without giving it a thought. Never mind that there was something Oriental about their sweaty faces. But nobody in their right mind would call them *Soviets*. Soviets? Bollocks. The word smacked of propaganda. But who was behind the propaganda anyway, who generated it? And what was it they were trying to propagate and to whom? We were all in the same boat. In me personally the communists never took any interest. Why would the communists have been interested in me? They included blokes who had grown up in my street, we used to kick the ball around together when we were young, and mock everyone who wouldn't join in. Anyone who didn't play football was a wimp in my book.

My younger son was walking along the street with a pretty woman.

Incidentally, he's never been interested in football.

And yet – he's the spitting image of me now! Mind you, my face hasn't always been chubby and even today it may not be as fat as his.

I bet he can't stand his own face.

I put a lot of effort into making that kite. It was large and lozenge-shaped, made of paper and sticks. It had a long tail that got entangled in a gooseberry bush right away and as I tried to free it scraps of paper were caught on the bush. My younger son found this as distressing as when he saw me butchering a chicken for the first time. I never really enjoyed slaughtering poultry but my sons thought I did. I'm sure my younger son reviled me, I'm less sure if my older son did, he may not have been as harsh. It's even possible that he loved me, in a feeble, self-conscious young-man sort of way.

He loved me but I've messed everything up.

I took him along to the hardware shop and got him enrolled as an apprentice. That's how he came to witness my flings with female colleagues. He found this humiliating. To add insult to injury, the boy had always had a slight stammer. I admit it was a mistake to try to make him a sales assistant. But who doesn't make a mistake once in a while. I wanted him to become a sales assistant, to be like his father. But could he ever have been like me? I'm a totally different kind of person. I'm made of different stuff. It was absolute hell for him to be in the shop with me. Everyone constantly had their eyes on him and felt sorry for him. It's the young, unmarried son rather than his father who's meant to flirt with shop assistants his age! But all the girls, even the youngest ones, only had eyes for me. He'd been pushed aside as far as girls were concerned. A bashful, shy, quiet son, even if he's quite good-looking, doesn't stand a chance on his father's turf, especially when his father's the boss. Perhaps if a girl with a lot of empathy, a romantic soul, the saviour type, had happened to be around... His mother had been that exact type! But my older son wasn't lucky enough to meet a kind girl who might have relieved him of his fear, and maybe also of his virginity. Once, just as I was busy lavishing attention on an apprentice, one of his classmates, my son walked in and saw everything. He backed away at once, slamming the door shut. He didn't say a word about it at home. There would have been no point. My wife was convinced I was cheating on her anyway, even before I really started to cheat on her, and she didn't need material proof or witnesses, at some point she just began to take my infidelity for granted. She thought infidelity was second nature to me. My son's testimony wouldn't have added to the number of our rows and her jealous scenes. He had weighed it all up and arrived at the right conclusion: to keep mum. I realize that this made him even more depressed but what was I to do? I'm not a psychologist! Besides, a proper son would have shown some understanding for his father, he would surely have rooted for me. Males ought quite naturally to bond together against women, to scheme! How was I supposed to save my family if the males in it weren't pulling at the same end of the rope? And even if I stopped having flings my wife wouldn't have believed it. She would never have known because she never talked to anyone so how would she have found out? She hadn't heard any of the gossip about me, yet she took it for granted even before gossip started doing the rounds.

The apprentice had a pretty, girlish face, and it aroused me. Lips glistening with saliva, delicate skin on her cheeks, soft, down-like facial hair you can't quite feel with your fingers but can just about see with your eyes, oh yes, there it is. She was lying on the counter on a pile of invoices with me bending over her just as my older son opened the door. He backed out, which suggests that he'd seen and understood everything. Nevertheless, not only did he never let slip about this at home, he never mentioned it to me either. I realize that this was the only sensible response in his situation. I have no idea what our conversation about this incident might have been like, had it ever taken place. I think the reason such inconceivable conversations never take place is precisely because they are inconceivable. And as for my younger son, he knew nothing about this but hated me anyway. But at the same time his mother drove him mad with her constant talk of infidelity, he couldn't stand it. He thought he didn't need a reason to hate me.

"No, please don't," the apprentice said, trying to dampen my ardour and pushing my hands away from her unbuttoned blouse. But in reality she was loving it. She assumed that being the object of her boss's exclusive attention was something she ought to be happy about. She had no idea that virtually the entire female staff of our little shop in the main street had enjoyed my attentions. I still run into some of them in the street sometimes. And I wonder if they're having it off with anyone. I doubt it. Most of them are of pensionable age now. They're certainly not having it off with me. I've been faithful to the woman for whom I eventually left my wife. Actually, that's not quite it: I left my wife because she had failed as a wife. She had brought her future solitude upon herself.

I'm innocent.

I have built a family nest, it's fallen apart but hey, there are loads of people who've never built anything in their lives! Compared to them I'm in the clear. One of those who've never built anything in their life is my younger son. And talking of fidelity and infidelity: can you be unfaithful when you're old and tired? It's easy for us, elderly men. Exhaustion turns us into morally impeccable citizens. That is why we demand to be respected. Fortunately, few people realize that it's not a demand that's justified.

* * *

My wife was prancing around me, waving her arms in front of my face. Her fury made me shudder, I ducked in panic but there was a wall behind me and I bruised myself really badly. I was unable to help my wife, I didn't know how to calm her down, she wouldn't listen to me, well, actually I didn't say anything, I lacked the right words but even if I had said something she wouldn't have taken any notice.

My son came out of his room.

He looked annoyed but not shocked.

What he saw fitted in with his idea of us. It just annoyed him. Our fighting annoyed him. That was all there was to it. How can a child be so insensitive towards his parents? Why, that's worse than if he'd shunted us into an old people's home. Our fighting had evidently distracted him from something. He went back to his room. I heard the sound of the typewriter. Great! His parents are at each other's throats and their son is taking notes. I got mad: was he hoping to capitalize on our situation? Did he think it was funny? My arm shot up and I slapped my wife across the face, screaming *stop it!* She kicked me in the knee, lost her balance and fell onto a rug.

Oh well, the fight is obviously coming to an end.

I run off to the garage.

I'm innocent.

But what about my son?

* * *

One night we were woken by a terrible clap of thunder or rumbling. The whole house shook, then silence fell. It turned out that the plaster had come off an entire outside wall, burying our neighbour's ornamental bushes under a layer of dust and debris half a metre thick. I'd never replastered a wall, I didn't have the strength. I contemplated leaving, disappearing and these thoughts paralysed me. The wall was damp just like the rest of the house, the basement was always at least ankle-deep in water. Gases welling up from the depths made the surface of the *Hwergelmir* whirl about so that it seemed as if the water was boiling. Slimy bugs had made the walls their home, slithering up along the pipes into the house. They would often wander onto the terrace, carelessly exposing themselves to the sun, which killed them. They dried up and lay there motionless and when my wife swept the terrace they turned into dust, making a quiet crackling sound as their dry antennae whirled in the air glittering like the long silvery eyelashes of oriental dancers before landing in the yard where they mingled with the clay or vanished in the grass.

* * *

"I know you're annoyed with your father," said the man who had come to see my younger son. My son offered him a seat in his office. The man explained that he wanted to buy my car and trailer but knew that after my hasty departure all the paperwork for the trailer had been left in the house in Lovecká Street.

"I know you're annoyed but you're making a mistake," the man went on. "Hatred will come back to haunt you.

It's unfair to be judgmental... Your daddy has never hurt you so you shouldn't judge him! Also, he feels sorry for your mother. He feels sorry about what has happened to her."

"Has something happened to her?"

"Certainly."

"And he feels sorry about that? Doesn't he realize that he was the reason that something happened to her? That is, assuming that anything did."

"Don't be like that. You must have noticed her condition, you weren't a baby after all."

"What condition?"

"You know, in the basement."

"She had a condition in the basement?"

"Yes, when she dug up the floor down there."

"We had a burst pipe so she had to dig it up. Who else was supposed to do it – my father? He was sulking in the garden or in the garage. Or do you mean the digging in the basement earlier? During the alterations? But that time they did the digging together, my dad and mum! My dad's brother, the one who had built the house, had built the basement so low you could hardly stand there upright. All mum and dad did was make it deeper. Is that what you had in mind? Other than that I don't know what strange condition in the basement you might be talking about."

"I see, so your daddy did some digging in the basement as well?"

"Didn't he tell you? He did, initially. Before he started throwing tantrums. But until then he did some digging as well. My daddy…if that's what you'd like to call him. And that something had happened to my mother? She sacrificed herself for her children – that's what happened to her! But my father couldn't understand that because the only sacrifices he was prepared to make were in his own interests."

"There you go again! Being judgmental! You don't appreciate the complexities of life."

My younger son had no idea who he had the honour of dealing with, even though Mr Labadaj, who later told me about their meeting, used to be a frequent visitor at the house in Lovecká Street. Admittedly, that was a long time ago. Once I'd invited this erudite man, he might even have been a professor, to come and see if there was anything he could do about my wife. About her and that pagan cult of hers. By the way, a couple of Jehovah's Witnesses rang my bell yesterday. My new wife opened the door. There was a retarded looking chap standing outside, accompanied by another, younger one. I told myself straight away that something had to be done to rescue the youth from the retard. The retard asked politely if they could bother us for a moment. And had I noticed the negative developments in our country. Deteriorating interpersonal relations and the like. And various natural omens.

I turned to the youth and said: "Who's this guy with you? You've got to free yourself of him or he'll destroy your life forever. Get rid of the fucker! You still have a chance." The boy took offence. The retard was totally unperturbed. So I slammed the door shut and that's when I thought of my former wife. Suddenly I felt proud of her: she'd chosen a solitary path rather than group hysteria. Because group hysteria is always ready to pounce, it comes in many and varied forms, you encounter it at every turn and if you have serious problems it's a miracle if you don't succumb to it.

My request with regard to my wife and her pagan cult took Mr Labadaj aback. "I had no idea these kinds of problems also occur in this country. And in an ordinary working class family at that!" he exclaimed. Later, as he bent over a crack in the basement concrete, he stated: "Your wife is developing...let's put it this way...a peculiar kind of relationship with the netherworld. Most probably it's her way of compensating for your failed marital bond. And that's not to your liking. Do you think that's the right attitude to have?"

His critical tone came as a nasty surprise to me.

"You must understand that you've deprived your wife of the kind of security that is so important to a woman. Marriage is the cornerstone of everything. It's the foundation of life, a ritualized, sacred thing. I'm sure it's never occurred to her to look for anything else. For another cornerstone. And as a result of the de facto disintegration of your marriage – because your marriage has ceased to function – she has nothing left to lean on. Have you seen the Germanic god in the basement?" asked Labadaj, rubbing his jaw with his thumb and index finger.

"You can't be serious! If I'd seen some god I wouldn't have asked you to come. My wife is off her rocker, that's what this is about."

"Well then, what would you have done if you had seen the god? I'd really like to know! Would you believe in it if you saw it?"

"Now that's a tough one! If I saw a god? I would accept his existence. I would accept the Catholic god, too. I have seen the communists but I wouldn't say that I believe in them. I don't understand what you mean by believing. When I see a table and I'm aware of its existence, does it mean I believe in it?"

"How can we be sure that we're dealing with a Germanic god? What if he's, let's say, Slavonic? Or Czechoslovak? Or purely Slovak? If you and I spotted a being emerging from a crack in the concrete – shrouded in smoke and vapour...do you have a stool somewhere around here?"

"You can sit down here at the desk, let me just wipe the dust off the chair. Can I offer you a drink?"

"Do you have any vintage Alibernet?"

"I've got beer. Golden Pheasant. I don't drink myself but I always have a couple of bottles in. My wife...well, she does have a drink sometimes."

"Here we go. You're doing everything you can to hurt her. Why do I, a virtual stranger, need to know that your wife is a beer drinker?"

"I wish it was just beer."

"You've got a nerve! It's like her telling somebody that you have a small pecker!"

"That's a bad example. She would never say anything about peckers."

"What's more important is why you're trying to deprive your wife of her basement cult. It seems perfectly innocent to me. Just a vicarious activity…"

"But her mental health is at stake!"

"Don't you think happiness is more important than mental health?" Labadaj exclaimed sternly.

"My wife has been telling this nonsense to our neighbours. People are becoming frightened of her. Not in a respectful kind of way but the way you're frightened of a lunatic because you can never be sure what they might get up to next."

"But she needs this cult to suppress her anxiety about the disintegration of your marriage."

"Why do you keep going on about the disintegration of our marriage?"

"Don't be ridiculous. Honestly – do you think there's anyone in this town who's not aware what sort of person you are? In fact, your wife might be the only one who's not sure about that, and maybe your sons aren't either. Your younger son at least. Because the older one…"

"So my colleague Drdavá has provided you with detailed information."

"Mrs Drdavá has provided me with factual information."

"I don't want my marriage to disintegrate!" I yelled.

To be honest, the main thing I cared about was having some peace and quiet. This is how I would like things to be: my wife at home looking after the children, saying nothing, not reproaching me for anything, making no demands of me, while I go to work, have a good time there and after a pleasant day spent with a nice team and enjoying some minor flings I go back home and there she is waiting for me, asking no questions, serving dinner, the boys playing in the living room while I look in on them and get over the brief awkward moment. Because, let's face it, we've got nothing to say to each other, but what am I to do? None of my friends in Fatranská Street ever talked to their fathers. They just took orders and reported on how they carried them out. That's how things used to be. Our fathers...ageing, worn out men...peasants, workers, drunks...that was the norm! Even today watching old films about building socialism makes me feel ill. The films show our fathers. What did they look like? What was eating away at their ugly mugs? What kind of leprosy? Some sort of general socialist smallpox? The regime's psoriasis? The fathers and sons of our era passed each other in Fatranská Street in silence. At most the fathers would bark an order or give us a good whack. That was it. Whenever I looked in on them, my sons would lower their eyes. They felt guilty, it's only natural for a son facing his father to feel inadequate and awkward, a son should never forget that the reason he can't get on top of something is because he's not trying hard enough.

"I can't see anything out of the ordinary here," professor Labadaj noted, leaning on the *Yggdrasil*. "I can't even detect any smell of sulphur. Naïve people believe that godlessness and heresy are inextricably linked with the smell of sulphur. Similar to the foul smell in the thermal baths at Dudince. But that would suggest that evil has healing properties. Like a natural spring! Don't get me wrong but, to be honest with you," the professor looked at me intently before concluding, "I think you're a nasty piece of work. Who are you trying to convince that your wife communicates with Germanic mythological beings? Where would she have even got such an idea? And where did you get it, that's what I'd like to know. Look, if you want my advice, kindly accept that your wife is unhappy and that's all there is to it. You've destroyed her. These things happen. The world is a cruel place. As long as mankind is divided into two sexes, war and natural selection will rage between them. And war and natural selection are invariably followed by coupling, by procreation of the winners, that is to say the losers of the future. That's how nature intends it, although normally nature doesn't act intentionally. Nature is an unfeeling automaton. In fact, bringing feeling into it is pointless. After all, we wouldn't dream of accusing a corpse of being unfeeling. Nature is a corpse on life support, but luckily euthanasia is within reach. So let's not blame nature. Although you would blame anyone, wouldn't you? Just so you can stay

~ 62 ~

blameless. You and I could be friends, go out for a cup of tea or coffee. I get it, you don't drink alcohol. Evil people don't need drugs to become intoxicated, they are intoxicated with themselves. Just look at your eyebrows. They're joined! They form a thick black line across your forehead, a dark line. If I could feel your skull...maybe I'll get a chance one day...when we get to know each other better...I'd be able to tell you more about yourself, based on the shape of your skull. In the late nineteenth and early twentieth century there were certain branches of science... But after Hitler lost the war, some fascinating scientific findings became unacceptable. If only I could feel your skull! If only I could pass the end of my index finger along the ridge of your brow! I could read you like an open book! By the way, have you ever heard of Baldur?"

"He's our new neighbour, he's just started building a house across the street from the Ember family."

"No, no, Baldur is the most beautiful, purest and youngest of the Germanic gods. It could easily be you, don't you think? A vestige of the god's name in your surname suggests this. I'm sure there are times you picture yourself as a young god. You have all the prerequisites... And talking about imagination: meanwhile, in your wife's eyes you've turned into that Slavonic black god, Černobog. That's exactly what's suggested by that unfortunate monobrow of yours."

* * *

"You know what's terrible?" I asked Labadaj in the basement at Lovecká Street.

The professor waved his hand dismissively and squeezed himself behind the stove, where he discovered a symbol, partly obscured by two red pipes.

"My wife has no idea what this house has been built for. My sons don't suspect anything either."

"You're not talking about what's behind the door now, are you?" Labadaj looked at me with a sneer.

"Behind the door?" I asked, blushing.

"I bet this piece of apparatus – because you're the only one who calls this a *house* – hasn't been built for the sake of what you've been keeping behind the door. Whoever constructed this apparatus had a different purpose in mind. You're to blame for whatever is behind that door. You think your wife is crazy? You've got some nerve! You know very well you've never given her half a chance. You and that Drdavá! And that experiment of yours! Let's go!" Without waiting to see if I was following he started walking down the corridor to the right, deeper into the basement. We reached a metal door.

"The key," he said.

I reached into my pocket without thinking.

"See?" he looked at me as if I was a small boy caught masturbating. I handed him the key. He opened the door. We entered. A strange smell knocked us back. We heard rustling in a corner behind a pile of coal.

"This is all your fault! Your colleague Drdavá is just a

medium but you are the instigator."

It was there, whining in the corner.

Words fail me.

"Pass me a stake and some garlic!" Labadaj ordered.

"I haven't got any."

"You moron!" he hissed. "Then why did you bring me here?"

* * *

"My father has never hurt us? You can't be serious!" my younger son snapped at Labadaj. He was standing in the middle of the office, looming above the professor who sat in an armchair next to a conference table.

"You were almost an adult when your father left. You must have realised by then that he did it for your own good," Labadaj replied. "In order to put an end to the endless arguments. Not arguments really, more like monologues. Your mummy's hysterical monologues. That environment was toxic for everyone!"

"Oh, so it was for our own good that we were left practically penniless for years on end? That's when the revolution happened. The Revolution!" My younger son gave a sarcastic laugh.

"Your daddy provided for you. He left you the house!"

"This daddy, as you call him, claimed he'd left everything behind but he kept coming back for one thing after another. In the end he even took the car. After he left us, he seemed illuminated by joy out there, after he ditched us and all responsibility for his actions. The day he left my mother I happened to be sitting out on the terrace. The door opened all of a sudden and there he was in the doorway with a large suitcase I'd never seen before even though I had the contents of all the wardrobes and all the hiding places under the beds thoroughly mapped out! That moment...as he passed me carrying his suitcase...his greyish, pallid face angry, his brow furrowed – pretending to be lost in thought, looking for a solution! Plus he was unshaven, as if to suggest he couldn't even get a shave as long as he lived with us in this wretched house, as if the very mirror in the bathroom repelled him, you know I still use that mirror in the flat, it's been good enough for me, isn't that funny, it's still good enough for me, after all these years! My father even hated the soap he used to lather up with his shaving brush, he hated the shaving brush with its purplish-red handle, he even hated the fact that I had also started shaving. That I had grown up. He would stand behind me watching the tiny lacerations in my skin as a wound opened amid the soft hairs, at first I felt no pain but then it started to sting, it's to make sure you don't slash your throat by mistake, he said, but the way he watched me was different, it wasn't a caring, pro-tective look, it was more as if he wanted to deprive me of something. Aftershave made the stinging worse. And he just stood there watching me. He wanted to claim the credit for something nature provided. Those tiny stinging grazes from shaving… The sensation of adulthood. Yes, a sensation that was very much my own. Something you experience only once in a lifetime. You can only relish it once. He was on the lookout for this sensation. This thing, this exclusive domain of youth, that's what he wanted to experience again! And what happened after that? That moment… That's the moment I've been meaning to tell you about. As he opened the terrace door and banged into the doorway with that unfamiliar suitcase, there was a bang! That moment, as he went past me and the awful suitcase brushed against my knees, forgive me, but I've never been able to see anything good or beneficial in that moment!"

"Take it easy. Don't get upset. An intelligent person should always maintain an unbiased perspective. I know your daddy thought about you a lot. It wasn't easy for him to leave. He'd made a number of attempts to salvage the situation. So that you could continue as a family."

"My father never gave us a moment's thought. It seemed as if he was constantly lost in contemplation but the only thing on his mind was his own problems. He never took account of our situation. The situation of his wife and children."

"Do you think he didn't suffer?"

"Of course he suffered! And how he paraded his suffering! But only for his own sake. He was an individualist and egotist even before he knew what those terms meant. I'm sure he's familiar with them now, I hear he's been doing a lot of reading. He has left it rather late. While he still lived with us he made do with the communist party's daily. I'm told he now drinks whisky and has been known to light a cigar."

"You've got to understand him. After all those years of self-sacrifice he finally felt he gained the freedom he'd been deprived of when he was young. That was partly his own fault for having married so early. But I see in this an appreciable sense of responsibility, don't you agree? And he doesn't smoke or drink – those were just short-lived experiments."

Mr Labadaj was convulsed by a coughing fit as he was telling me this.

We were sitting in the kitchen, wondering what could have got into my younger son. My new wife brought us some biscuits and lemonade.

Does my younger son have *any* idea of who his father actually is?

Does he really know the man he'd seen only with the eyes of a child as he was growing up?

In his adolescence he wouldn't talk to me at all. Now he thinks I wasn't interested but the fact is he was impossible to talk to. I know that adolescents are generally difficult to get on with, an obedient child might suddenly turn into an adolescent and then that's it, but my relationship with my younger son had never really worked.

* * *

The mummy is propped up against the gas meter outside the house as I arrive home from work, actually I'm coming home from school, nonsense, not from school, or maybe I am coming from school after all, either way, it's there as I'm walking along the tarmac down Lovecká Street, though when I was at school it was a meadow, there was no tarmac, no houses. I stop in front of the mummy. It's my wife. I shouldn't actually know her at this point, I'm just a little brat, a promising young football player, and yet I do know her and we're married, in the illogical nature of dreams it's my wife with her arms folded across her chest swaddled in layers of petrified bandages, she's propped up against the wall, the strands of her thin, mussed up hair stand on end as if carrying an electric charge, her mouth is open, I can't see her eyes, it's all just a blur where they should be.

The thing I'm standing before is waiting for me, a schoolboy with a satchel, and I'm scared, more scared than ever before.

I don't like talking about dreams.

What my mummy dream told me – dreams always tell us something – was that I had hurt my wife, I'd destroyed her, shackled her to her children, it should definitely have been someone else who had fathered her children, someone older, more responsible, someone who'd have respected her, who'd have been happy to have her for a wife. What my dream communicated – dreams always communicate something – was that my wife would die and that I'd be responsible for her death. She did, indeed, die later on but I don't feel responsible, it's my younger son who should feel responsible. I'm saying this based on what the young woman who bought the house in Lovecká Street told me. I met her once. Several times, actually. She told me some fascinating things: it turned out she knew the circumstances of my former wife's death, having learned them from my younger son. I don't want his story to overshadow mine but in his version his mother suddenly lost her memory at the end of an unusually harsh winter early in the new millennium. One might have expected the world to go up in flames but in those days it seemed, rather, that a new ice age was looming, and to cap it all the heating in the house in Lovecká Street had broken down. It was then that my ex-wife had lost her memory and put far too much salt in the soup, she had no memory of putting any salt whatsoever in the soup, in fact she was about to put in some more salt, another generous measure, having already forgotten that she'd seen my son push his plate away in disgust only a moment earlier. In those days she would spend all day sitting in the kitchen on a low chair by the window, in semi-darkness, with the curtains drawn, she'd stare at the table, the sideboard and the stove sitting there all curled up, but in fact she was just staring into the void, her eyes gleaming in the reflection of the lamp in my younger son's room, where he was reading, the blare of the music couldn't drown out the profound silence in the kitchen, this was the state she was in, this loneliness in a darkness she had embraced of her own accord, in which she used to constantly remind our sons, both of them, that they hadn't done anything to save her. She won't even eat a crust of bread, let alone any meat, damn it, she won't eat any potatoes or rice, she hasn't eaten for weeks and never goes to the toilet, my older son insisted to my younger one, I've been watching her, he said, sounding upset, I've been watching her and I know she hasn't been once. And he really did watch her, he was stuck at home, too, being unemployed he had plenty of time and he was able to watch her. Who was going round the bend here? Was it a lunacy contest? For her it was a way of dealing with the broken toilet flush, which neither of my sons was able to fix and they couldn't afford to buy a new flush so she had gone into a sulk and abandoned her basic bodily functions. I never imagined such a thing was possible, my younger son said in astonishment in the presence of the young woman who bought the house in Lovecká Street, but apparently it was, and my sons felt awfully hurt by her determination, they were convinced that this was what it was all about, that she was out to hurt them. One day my younger son came home to find her in the corridor looking a total mess, with her cardigan buttoned askew, its front tucked in and its back hanging out of her track-suit which she had put on inside out, her eyes like small turbid puddles. My younger son spoke to his mother and told her she looked a dreadful mess and asked her why she was standing there, but instead of replying she asked what she was supposed to do, as she had forgotten the things she'd been doing all her life. On another occasion my younger son came home to find her sitting on the low chair by the kitchen window in semi-darkness, with her back to the drawn net curtains as well as the drapes, close to the sideboard, from which all kinds of odds and ends had suddenly come tumbling out onto the carpet. My younger son clutched his head, what do you need all this stuff for, it will all come in handy one day, she explained, but she had no idea when it might come in handy, this was stuff she'd picked up outside the house and in the street, some things she'd found in rubbish bins, back when she was still strong enough to go out she used to collect rubbish and store it in the sideboard, something had to be done about that, so my two sons had a serious talk about it. The next day my older son went with his mother to see our GP, telling him that his mother was confused and kept forgetting things, and that on top of everything else she'd started collecting junk, the doctor referred his mother to a psychiatrist who concluded that this wasn't a case for him so they passed her on to the hospital where the confused woman was subjected to painful tests, like having her stomach prodded for no obvious reason, then they put her through her paces in the cancer ward and discovered that she was riddled with tumours although they couldn't locate the primary source of the malignant growth, whether it was in her brain,

lungs or another part of her body altogether, and through-
out the examination they made no bones about the fact
that this lady stood absolutely no chance whatsoever and
so eventually they all agreed that she should be discharged.
So my older son brought her back home, by then you
could see through her and she could barely walk, moving
only very slowly if at all, instead of on the carpet she
walked above it, immediately above it, hovering above
the carpet and the floor that was covered in dust and
rubbish, she'd long given up the struggle to keep the
house tidy and to maintain normal relations with her sons
or with other people and objects, she didn't even have
the strength to observe the laws of physics. Her neighbour
Mrs Ičová could say a thing or two about that, she was
the only friend who had stuck with her almost to the end,
they would sit together in the blacked-out kitchen as
Ičová gently tried to nudge her back to her senses with
a few kind words but even in the semi-darkness she could
see that the old woman was far, far gone, she was most
at ease in the company of ghosts, especially those of her
parents who had died in the eighties, she would talk to
them, Ičová would hear all sorts of things and it didn't
escape her attention that one day the low chair by the
kitchen window on which the unfortunate old woman
used to sit stopped creaking although nobody had fixed
it or propped it up in any way, nobody had driven the
nails further into the wood, it was just that the woman
had rapidly lost weight although her shape hadn't changed,

it was just that she had shrunk internally. My younger son was worried that he would end up inhaling her and never breathe her out again, that he would lose his mother by breathing her in, but this notion was most likely inspired by the fact that my younger son had suffered from respiratory problems ever since he was a little boy, he was only worried about himself, not his mother, he dreaded the thought of choking on his mother, he wasn't really worried about her, there was no real need because worrying is just a way of casting a spell, an attempt to avert danger but the danger she faced was by then unavoidable. Later on she would just lie on her bed huddled between sheets, duvet covers, pillows, tattered yellowing duvets in clashing colours which she'd found and thrown together without rhyme or reason. Dirty wet towels, blankets and throws lay scattered on the floor around the bed and on top of chairs and the old sewing machine, and as days went by, my wife had less and less idea where she was, who she was, what she was for but, then again, does anyone have a really good idea of themselves, can anyone be one hundred per cent certain, has anyone never, ever been plagued by doubts, my younger son asked the young woman who'd bought the house in Lovecká Street? His mother no longer cared about the extraordinary mess through which my older son waded noiselessly, fetching a variety of containers, jugs, pots and bowls large and small, to wash the used rags, nappies and sheets, awkwardly and without any tangible result and then spread them out to dry on radiators and pipes that carried heat from the basement, except that there was hardly any heat to speak of since the heating had broken down, the only heat came from an improvised, second-hand replacement stove attached to the pipes of the long-broken-down heating system. My older son directed the smoke into the pipes and stoked the fire with bits of wood and rubbish, most of the smoke would leak out of the badly sealed joints, billowing around the house, and bursting out whenever my older son opened the window, which happened very rarely because he didn't want to let the outside world in, he was scared of the outside world, he preferred to be locked up in this limbo where the struggle for the time and manner of his mother's death was being waged. My older son did everything he could, I have to give him credit for that, he tried to make his mother's end easier but he didn't prove quite up to it even though he was surprisingly strong-willed. When he did open the window, the draught would catch hold of the nappies, peeling off thin, brownish-yellow slivers of dried-on stool and disproving the claim that the old woman's metabolism was no longer functional, the stuff now came streaming out of her non-stop as if what remained of her innards was trying to get out of her, evacuate and escape from this house, even though she wasn't accepting any food but maybe her stomach was processing the substance of the body that encased it, that was the only explanation my older son could come up with. The nappies, trailing their dried-up excrement, rose up on the draught and flew out of the open window, finding refuge on electric pylons. My older son kept going down to the basement and there, gasping for breath, he would chop pieces off the *Yggdrasil* to stoke the fire in the stove, eventually chopping up the entire tree in the smoky basement, and as he did so, he saw ghosts, of course he would, he wasn't blind, but he put it down to being dazed and exhausted. All day long he would potter about the flat that reeked of illness, going from room to room lugging around the wet, dirty towels, used sheets and motley duvet covers, trying to separate the soiled ones from those that were even more soiled, he would run a bath and wash them by hand pouring white washing powder into the cold water, the house was cold even though it was early spring, he would bend over the bathtub, then walk over to the window and stare at the windows of the house opposite but never spotted anyone, it was impossible to see anyone as the glass had always been opaque, another reason why it had never been even remotely possible to spot anyone, in any case the house next door was quite far away, the plot was quite wide on that side, and in addition there was the land belonging to the other house, an empty old hovel, which stood at the far end. My older son shivered with cold, he thought of the heating tank in the basement, of the fire going out, he felt trapped and yet he didn't run away, will anyone ever appreciate that? He didn't run away until some time later. He put up with looking after his deranged, dying mother until the very end, becoming intimately acquainted with the failing human body, its fragile, defunct nature, its alienness and futility, this body can't possibly have been you, mum, he whispered, this body can't be mother, the only thing this body might be is the instigator of a new body, mine, but I'm at odds with my own body. My older son had never wanted anything to do with his body, it felt just as alien to him as that of the mother he was looking after, encased as she was in her dry, taut skin, greyish here, yellowish-brown there, the skin also formed a part of the body it encased, he spent night after night sitting by the body, sometimes he saw his mother stand up and float around the flat like a feather, lightly gliding on the draught along the walls and the furniture.

And what did my younger son do in the meantime?

He was hiding in the pub.

He was telling his friends how he suffered because his mother was dying.

His friends sympathized and shared their stories of their mothers dying.

My younger son was furious.

He jabbed at the ice at the bottom of his glass of Fernet and coke with the straw.

He was fucking angry.

Why should he be looking after a dying woman?

This was what infuriated him.

Maybe he didn't notice that it was in fact my older son who was looking after her.

I wish I had been the one dying, he said to the young woman who bought the house in Lovecká Street.

How could my younger son have turned out so differently from my older one?

My older son is capable of love and compassion, even though these are exactly the qualities my ex-wife and I almost destroyed in him, we never had any patience with him, we were irritated by his speech defect, my wife often shouted at him, stop muttering, what language is that supposed to be? Is it Slovak or Hungarian? It freaked her out. I was slightly better at controlling myself but even I flew off the handle a few times, actually, maybe that time it was me who shouted at him, I'm not sure, but who cares? On the other hand, I'm quite sure a child can't have anything that important to say, so I didn't really pay him any attention, I had other things on my mind.

My older son looked after his dying mother despite the painful memories of being shouted at, which made his stammer even worse. When he was older he preferred to keep quiet, keeping quiet even as he and his brother handed their mother's clothes to some dimwit at the morgue who was supposed to take care of the deceased, put some decent clothes on her *body*, the two of them stood there before this clown who was evidently incapable of even taking care of himself as far as clothes were concerned, I'll get her dressed properly, don't you worry, the scarecrow assured them, they handed him a bag with a crumpled blouse and skirt, this was what my older son had found in his mother's wardrobe, a crumpled blouse and a skirt, thanks, said the dimwit taking the bag and shoving it under his arm so that even if the blouse and the skirt hadn't already been crumpled, they would have got crumpled now, the dimwit thrust out his palm towards them with an apologetic smile as if someone else had forced him to thrust his palm out, as if his palm had been thrust out in front of him against his will, and my younger son put a hundred note in it. My younger son covered all the expenses relating to the funeral, not because he was selfless but because my older son had no job, he didn't have a penny, a cent, not a bean as they say, that might have changed later, after he vanished, leaving my younger son the empty house, he must have found a job somewhere, perhaps he got rid of his speech impediment, too, a speech impediment is more likely to disappear than asthma or diabetes, incidentally, as far as I'm concerned, my health has been almost perfect so far, apart from a problem with my gall bladder. The dimwit with the bag under his arm said goodbye and disappeared down the pathology department corridor. My younger son voiced his suspicion, which he later repeated to the young woman who bought the house in Lovecká Street, that as soon as the dimwit turned the corner, he tossed the bag with the clothes into a bin with patients' cut-off body parts, arms, legs and appendixes, my younger and older son then went for a beer, they felt that haggling with the dimwit was a great and exhausting achievement for which they deserved some alcohol, some fun, in short, to flush away the tensions and strains of the days they had been through.

Later, when my older son was clearing out the basement, he liberated the roots and the tree trunk from the concrete, what was it that was growing here anyway, he asked my younger son, some kind of oak tree or what? My younger son just gave it an angry kick, that was all. The older one disposed of the roots that were left. But the branches still remained. They had grown into the walls and they still hold the house in Lovecká Street firmly in their grip. I wonder how this will affect the life of the young woman who's bought the house and who later told me what my younger son had told her about his mother's death, and even though I don't want his story to overshadow mine, let me add that he told her that my older son really did everything in his power to look after his dying mother, even my younger son admitted as much, my older son had tried to ease the burden of her dying, since nobody expected her to survive, and as he eased the burden of her dying he took note of everything, registered all the attendant phenomena, even the seemingly insignificant details, the twitching of the curtains, the rustling under the bed, the draught that had no discernible source, the light effects, he recorded all the facts he had observed in big red notebooks, he made drawings of his mother's facial expressions, including the one she bore when he ran into her in the house in Lovecká Street shortly after her funeral, he saw her in the bedroom wandering past the wardrobes and the sofabed where she had lain while he looked after her, although he wasn't very good at looking after her but at least he tried, he hadn't run away like my younger son. My younger son couldn't cope with the situation, he was repelled by his mother and was equally repelled by the fact that he was repelled by her, he was repulsed by himself and swore he would commit suicide as soon as she died as a punishment for how he had behaved, besides, he didn't want to grow old and give someone – but whom? – the same kind of trouble as his mother had given him by growing old, decrepit and confused, except that, of course, my younger son has gone on living, his bad conscience following his mother's death soon evaporated, in fact he's been making ever more strenuous efforts to find someone who would look after him in his old age: on the lookout for a woman whom he could lumber with his person, since he has no children and can't count on any progeny to look after him.

He told the young woman who bought the house in Lovecká Street that his mother had spent her final days in a long nightdress, that was how he remembered her from his childhood when she used to wander around the house at night, checking that everything was in order, no window left open anywhere, she would also go out onto the terrace and stroke the cats sleeping curled up on the doormat, she believed the cats were the only creatures in the house in Lovecká Street that didn't cause her pain,

while my younger son regarded the cats as the only creatures that didn't cause *him* pain, so when his mother, as
she lay dying, mentioned the ginger tom who lived quietly
in the garage, and he realised that even on her deathbed
she was concerned about the tomcat, all of a sudden he
felt moved and overcome by such urgent affection for
the dying woman that he burst into tears. As he sat by
her bedside with his head in his hands he suddenly saw
his mother's face crumbling into another that seemed
more truthful and convincing, eventually turning into
the maternal face that he'd sought in vain in his mother's
visage ever since he was a small child, this face now rose
to the surface, engulfing the previous face and displaying
a surprising presence of mind, in the circumstances unexpected, even suspicious, as if for those few moments his
mother had suddenly gained access to a clear awareness
whose source was unambiguously somewhere outside
her body, perhaps outside of all bodies, and my younger
son heard his mother speak of rituals resurrected in the
basements and warehouses of our town, describe houses
skewered with *axis mundi* simulacra, like chunks of meat
on a spit, he heard her tell tales of wives abandoned and
humiliated by their husbands, women who meet in a café
on the corner of Lovecká Street, devotees of a powerful
cult who light torches and sacrifice lambs as male and
female students on the verge of adulthood ceremonially
smash dishes in the local grammar school's canteen, piec-
ing the shards together to fashion them anew, painting

them red and yellow, she told of curious seeds cast into the pagan soil of Europe, tiny, oddly disfigured bodies of uncertain provenance sizzling in pans and huge bonfires blazing in the middle of town squares. My younger son listened to his mother for a very long time but if he had heard anything more he never uttered a word about it to the young woman who bought the house in Lovecká Street, the only thing he ever admitted was that his mother's very last sentences seared horrendous scars into his memory that wouldn't disappear until he himself disappeared for good.

* * *

I have doubts about my new wife.

Did I say wife?

I should have said pensioner. I have aged, too. I might as well admit it. I'm too old to do another runner, though these days it's easy enough to escape, even abroad, you just pack your things and off you go, except that you'll still be stuck with the problem that is yourself and find it was pointless taking the risk of travelling by air even if you'd never even travelled by first class train before. I know there's no escape, so I might as well stay put. Sometimes it feels as if your life has been cast in stone. You can't subtract or add anything. After all, I tried for a long time to reach a state of finality. Now even the imperfections have become perfect and final. The wounds have been inflicted in all the right places. They hurt exactly the way they're supposed to. They won't heal because they're meant to stay open. They are what make me what I am, a wall outside, feelings inside, aroused by those who've ever had anything to do with me. All the feelings are still inside this person who's pieced together from what he has lived through. Only my sons popped out of me like stones from peaches after I left them with their mother all those years ago. But children belong with their mother, if you ask me. A father ought to be like a sailor, a Sindbad on the high seas. The trouble is, my wife lost her mind, the house had turned into a realm of hysteria and my younger son ruined the final years of his mother's life. He was the reason that they turned out to be final. Say what he will, however he spins it, it's inexcusable. He was incapable of looking after his mother, and he wasn't much help to his brother either. I think his mother died because in such circumstances she found it preferable to end the whole thing.

Or is it all my fault?

I was supposed to protect my wife from our badly brought up children.

Or could she be to blame?

She had raised the boys badly. I'm not the only parent after all.

Is anyone to blame at all?

I didn't go to her funeral because I had an inkling that it would end in a fiasco. I heard from an acquaintance that my sons didn't ask for a priest. My younger son was fiercely opposed to a religious funeral. Though I doubt that my wife would have wanted a priest at her funeral, I think that was just an idée fixe of this acquaintance of mine, she was convinced that all the women in Lovecká Street were devout. They may well be, but definitely not in this way.

I didn't see my wife's coffin.

I didn't see the woman lying in the coffin.

Her face, hips, breasts – in her case these all bore the stamp of death while she was still alive. I noticed this early on in our marriage. How many times do I need to repeat that I was never prepared for this sort of thing? Preparedness comes with experience. I resisted experiences, they caught me unawares, I was unable to react appropriately. As part of its moral fabric, society is duty bound to react appropriately to this kind of thing. In this sense I am immoral. Who will point their finger at me?

All this hastened my departure.

But that my departure should have hastened her death?

I categorically reject that!

The funeral procession that slowly wound its way around the graves towards a freshly dug hole comprised my wife's not very extensive family, village folk, unattractive men with a dignified gait and mostly repellent women in scruffy clothes with minds on their own business who kept casting discreet glances at their watches. When will this business finally end? It started drizzling, which annoyed everyone. Although you should always be prepared for it to rain at a funeral. I really hope that the number of mourners who turned up was sufficient to create at least the semblance of a procession. I'm sure they did turn up, just to see if I made an appearance. Would I have the cheek? They were hoping there would be a scandal. I'm sure my younger son would have assaulted me physically. I wonder what he was wearing: he had never worn a suit in his life, I'm positive he wouldn't have put on a suit, not even as a sign of respect for his mother. That just goes to show what sort of respect that was. I doubt that he has any respect for anyone. He's been a disgrace to me and I'm sure the funeral was no exception. So of course I didn't go! I didn't want to give him an excuse for a confrontation! But I know for a fact that most of those present would have taken my side. My wife's relatives liked me well enough when still I lived with her, I used to provide them with goods that were in short supply. All goods were in short supply in those days.

I'm sure my younger son wore an arrogant expression at the funeral. He wears his hatred on his sleeve, he believes hatred is a virtue. I presume that my older son withdrew into himself and just stood there in silence. Him I feel sorry for. I imagine he had real trouble communicating. I hope he didn't get too pissed before the funeral.

This acquaintance of mine told me that some shaman was hanging about the funeral. Allegedly he enacted a blood-curdling ritual behind the funeral chapel.

"A shaman? A ritual?" I asked her. "Do you have any idea what a shaman is and what a ritual is?"

She took offence.

But that doesn't mean that there hadn't been a ritual. The question is where the shaman had come from. I remembered my brother, I often think of him. The thing is, I didn't really have a brother when I was growing up. Instead someone to whom I had, for no reason whatever, referred as my brother, just turned up one day in order to fulfill his mission and build my house, only to disappear again afterwards.

A shaman?

He was expecting to meet me at the funeral. But at our age we should lower our expectations. Personally, I consider every day that passes without pain a miracle. I have no desire for any other woman. My current wife and I watch each other with mounting disgust, seeing two kinds of old age. What else is there to say? I am told my younger son has become a writer. I'm not interested in his scribblings. Although I do a lot of reading these days. But why should I care about his books? I'd only try to see if they say anything about me anyway, and I would never find anything, except maybe some stuff he's made up .

Sons don't know their fathers.

* * *

One more thing about Labadaj: could the thing my colleague Drdavá and I had summoned up be destroyed with a stake and a bit of garlic?

* * *

I'm hoeing the vegetable garden. My arms are still strong.

I'm thinking as I hoe. My memories of the period before the breakup with my late wife are remarkably scrappy. I guess I've suppressed them, all that's left are fragments, cliffs looming up from the grey sea of oblivion. This neurologist, I forget his name, I'll look him up in a minute – maybe it's the one who was always quoting Luria – once said that every time an impulse is discharged in our temporal lobe, similar to the minuscule cramps that occur in a stroke, it has some impact on our memory, on its deletion processes. As I stand here bent over the hoe I search for signs of minuscule cramps but find nothing.

It's not impossible that I experienced them once but I've forgotten.

They've vanished along with the years of my marriage.

I don't seem to recall many conversations occurring between me and my wife in those long-forgotten days. I used to feel mute, unable to put my feelings into words, to say anything about the pain I felt, if indeed I felt any pain at all. From time to time I had trouble with my gall bladder, I still do. I said nothing in my wife's presence, only occasionally berating her when her yelling went over the top and she whipped herself into frenzy. As a matter of fact, I also did some yelling.

It's coming back to me now, me yelling at her, then heading for the garage or the garden. What if, by chance, things were exactly the same then as they are now? Here I am, hoeing, again a married man, again embittered, again in the garden, with the house at my back. Could life be constantly repeating itself? No, that isn't true: I'm much older now and much more modest.

I no longer aim too high.

* * *

"Do come in," said Ľalika.

This happened a few months before I left the house in Lovecká Street for good. We sat down in the hallway, got talking, I complained about my wife. Ľalika remarked that her husband died two years ago but she was no longer in mourning. She showed me around her house and then we went down to the basement. Vapour from the leaking joints of the pipes rose ceiling-high. That's something I can't stand. Especially in such heat. I looked around the basement rooms and couldn't disguise my horror: "Everything here is exactly the same as in my house, except it's – the other way round! The other way round! Everything is the other way round!"

I ran down the corridor, turned a corner, looked around. And I saw my neighbour. A repulsive, fat, squat woman. Wide, fleshy face, crooked nose. And I saw the corridor. The corridor in the basement of my house turned right, this one turned left. I looked at the wall: in relation to the walls in my basement this was an anti-wall. I stamped my foot on the floor.

Anti-floor!

And I saw:

Anti-ceiling.

Anti-insects.

Anti-mice in anti-holes.

I also saw:

An anti-well.

I also saw:

Anti-stairs.

Anti-columns.

"Why, this is an anti-house!" I bounded over to my neighbour.

"Exactly."

"Anti-my-house!"

"That's correct."

"A spite-house!"

"You've put your finger on it."

"A spiteful anti-building!"

"You got it."

Ever since this house was built, nothing would work any longer. This house had turned my house into something completely ordinary that had no added value or special purpose. The meaning of life, which the very fact of dwelling in our house was supposed to have conferred on me and my family, had never existed. Our lives had been meaningless. Here, in the basement of this anti-house, I couldn't even derive any pleasure from the fact that we had, in reality, been living the same way as everyone else. Totally on our own. It had been up to us to fill our lives with meaning but we failed. All those years I was under the wrong impression that something important was happening and that we were a part of it, like lighthouse guards or shepherds looking after their herd.

"Who built this place?"

"Your brother."

"That's impossible!"

"But who else could have done it? The architect Kaššai? You know very well that he only designs town squares. And this is a work of art, built not just with the hands but also with the heart. This is not the kind of thing they teach at university. But maybe I'm not being specific and articulate enough. I'm just a stupid, fat woman with stubby legs. And cellulitis."

"My brother? But what was he trying to achieve?"

"Freedom. Freedom for all. Allowing our people to act as free individuals. To do only what they really wanted to do, of their own free will."

"If that's what he wanted to achieve all he had to do was not build my house."

"Yes, but he also needed the struggle! The tension! He had nobody to fight. I've already told you what I think of the standard of Kaššai's work. The air was meant to vibrate with tension, the house was meant to serve as the battleground of forces, energies, radiation. Haven't you noticed how in this town the hair on people's heads sometimes stands on end?"

"I thought it was just a fad. Something from the West. Like punk, maybe?"

"No, it's the tension! It manifests itself most frequently in young people, they are sensitive. But people like you barely have anything left to stand on end. Your brother thought about you a great deal. He was confused. He had built this exceptional house for you only to realize how indifferent was your attitude to life. Did you expect the house to do everything for you? Did you think you wouldn't need to do anything yourself? Your brother real-ised he had screwed up as far as the house was concerned. With regard to the townspeople, too. That is why he built an anti-house. He didn't tell you about it, he ran out of time. He died on the building site."

"You mean here?"

"No, on the third site."

"He started to build a third house? What on earth for?"

"As I said, he was confused. Once he completed my house he suddenly had pangs of regret. Not only had he deprived you and your family of the meaning of life but he'd also deprived himself of it: the two houses worked perfectly – in perfectly opposite ways – cancelling each other out. All of a sudden your brother became an or-dinary craftsman. So he embarked on a third project, a building that was intended to obliterate the humdrum equilibrium and serve as the first move in a new, exciting, perhaps even crazy game."

· "Where is this building?"

"He never finished it. There was an accident. An investigation was opened but it proved inconclusive. The building was later finished off by Kaššai, but only to Kaššai's standard. However, some of your brother's original intentions have been preserved, albeit in a muddled and flawed form. People living in that house tend to go out of their mind. Fortunately, in their case it's not all that obvious."

"So which house is it?"

"The big one in Podzámska Street."

"You mean the Communist Party headquarters?"

"Let's not get into that."

Ľalika stood there, with her flabby flesh, spongy shoulders, cylindrical fingers, teeth too big and eyes too small.

I said: "So all my life has been just slapstick."

"Whose life isn't slapstick? There are only two options: slapstick or tragicomedy."

"I've never taken a decision in my life."

"What about women? You do choose them. You pick this one or that..."

"I choose because I have to. I can't control myself. But what if I really want to be faithful? What if that's all I ever really wanted? Yes, it is! That's what I want! But some force keeps driving me."

"Your base instincts?"

"Yes, my base instincts."

"Oh well, these things happen."

"I'm unfree, empty, selfish!"

"Welcome to the club."

I looked around and saw an anti-club.

So the local populace hasn't been apathetic because of something actively radiated by my house. The people are apathetic because that's their nature. They let others trample all over them, they endure any regime without muttering a word, nodding meekly, raising their hands puppet-like to vote, and there isn't an iota of judiciousness in this, no Buddhist devotion, it's not the magical effect of my brother's apparatus, it's just their shitty slave mentality.

I noticed a familiar smell filtering into the basement air.

I was lost for words.

I reached a hand out to my neighbour.

"Keep your hands to yourself!" she shouted.

Who was she to shout at me like that? We weren't all that close.

BEFORE
THE BREAKUP

Miša discovered something in the flat.

It was behind the TV set in the corner of the living room. But later in the evening when she phoned Jano, who had left on a business trip a few days earlier, she made no mention of her discovery. Why make him worry? He had other things to worry about out there in that Asian metropolis. Or maybe he didn't? Doubt started gnawing at her: only the other night she'd dreamt of her husband in karaoke bars and the things he was getting up to with sluts; though they might go by a different, more posh name in those parts – Miša couldn't remember the precise word – she was quite sure they were just sluts, engaging in slutty practices.

After the routine call was over she sat in the kitchen until late at night, and as the light of a small lamp above the freezer illuminated her hands and fingers, and long shadows crept along the floor and the opposite wall, Miša wondered why this had to happen to her, of all people. Actually, not just to her, to Jano as well – but Jano didn't have an inkling of it. Or did he? Was he lying in a hotel bed somewhere with an inkling? Was he on the twentieth or thirtieth floor of a skyscraper, in the middle of negotiations, with an inkling?

Miša had grown up in a family where nothing ever appeared behind the TV set. Her parents had never even mentioned such a possibility to her, though they were happy to discuss in her presence the petty scandals involving their neighbours or people at work. But perhaps they'd had it in their bedroom too. Their daughter had never been allowed there. Could it have been in their bedroom? Did they take it along when they went on holiday? On one of those trips they used to take, leaving their daughter with her grandma in the country?

She went out into the hallway and called a friend from the landline, for she felt the need to discuss this unexpected problem with somebody. A few sentences into the conversation she replied, baffled:

"You mean I should go and see a psychiatrist?"

"Of course. You've got to. What if you're just imagining it all?"

"You mean...hallucinating? You really think I'm hallucinating?"

"But what if it isn't there at all? From what you're saying, it's almost the size of a wardrobe... Could something like that even fit behind the TV set?"

"Soňa, believe me, it's there!"

"I doubt it. Look, you know Dr Monty..."

"The one with the beard?"

"No, the one who goes to the Irish Pub."

"Where does he usually sit?"

"Right at the back, under the speakers."

"I don't know him at all."

"Well, then you must know the other one, what's his name...help me out..."

"You mean Dr Ráthé?"

"Exactly."

"But he's not a psychiatrist, he's a psychologist."

"All right, all right, a psychologist might do for starters..."

"What do you mean, for starters? It's as big as a wardrobe and you're calling this starters?"

"I've already told you there's *no way* it could be as big as a wardrobe. Just calm down. I'm sure it's much, much smaller."

"So how big do you think it is?"

"Let's agree it's the size of a matchbox, at most. It's absolutely tiny."

"Listen... How about you come and take a look?"

"That's out of the question. I can't."

"Why not? Do come! Please, help me!"

"But how? Is there really something wrong with you? What's this got to do with me? And anyway, I'm in a complicated situation."

"I don't understand."

"…"

"What is it? Can't you talk?"

"Erm…"

"All of a sudden. You can't talk just when I need you to do me a favour. Can't you even whisper?"

"I can do that. But what am I supposed to whisper? You'd better go and check again…"

"But I've been watching it the whole time. Actually… not the whole time, just now I was looking out of the window…and…by the entrance to the hairdresser's…you know where I mean…"

"Of course I do. By the entrance. So what's there?"

"There is…"

"Come on, what is it?"

"Nothing! Nothing at all! Don't you understand? It's not there. It's only here, behind the TV. Why don't I imagine it's out there, too, if I'm only imagining it? Let me tell you why: because it just isn't out there, only here. And you were lying."

"How was I lying?"

"When you said you could only whisper. Right now you were so curious about what was there by the entrance to the hairdresser's that you started shouting. Out of curiosity. And the only reason you found it so fascinating was because you have your hair done there yourself. So is the only time you're willing to listen to me, without accusing me of being crazy, when it involves you, too?"

The phone call ended on a rather uneasy note.

Miša sat down at the kitchen table, picked up a mirror and examined the pale skin of her pale face. It shone in the kitchen night. The eyes, the nose, the mouth, the corners of the mouth. Thoughtfully, Miša went on to examine her shoulders, chest, and legs. It would have been almost impossible to distinguish the whole from other wholes of this kind. Or perhaps only sometimes, thanks to the clothes, the situations in which they were discarded, by a particular whole's way of being naked. Way of being naked? Yes: see yourself for who you are! Step in front of the mirror, get to know yourself from the outside, but intimately! Let the inside follow. Follow the inside!

Miša stood up and sat down again.

She was sitting on her backside in the kitchen again.

Jano came home a few days later, dropped his bags in the hall, took off his shoes, went to the bathroom, had a shower, and, after thoroughly drying himself with a thick bath towel, headed for the living room. She was waiting for him by the door. Thinking of the sluts and the karaoke. And also of herself, her role. Was she supposed to float up into the sky, all dreamy-eyed and happy? Or should she let barbiturates, medication, or a psychiatrist take care of everything? She stepped back a little to let Jano pass. He sat down in the armchair and reached for the remote to switch on the TV. The flickering blue light carved objects out of the dark.

That's when Jano spotted it.

It was moving slowly, and in this slowness Miša detected both a sinister threat and something absolute. Jano didn't say anything. His face looked like a mask stretched on a rack of bone. Only when his wife whispered hysterically to him did he respond, commenting that, in his view, it made the living room even cosier than before, covering himself with his statement as though it were a precious Tibetan rug. Miša ran out of the block and called Soňa on her mobile. She was panting:

"I know everything!"

"What do you know?"

"It's turned up at your place too! That's why you can't talk! It's watching you! It's listening to you! It's growing!"

" ... "

"Do you have nothing to say to that???"

"I told you I can't talk."

"Well, whisper then."

"It's turned up here too. But it was a long time ago. It's stopped growing now, although, I admit, it's not getting any smaller either. We've got used to it. Just as it is. Look, I know how you feel. It's not easy to come to terms with the new situation at first... But is it really new? OK, I know you hadn't counted on it. You didn't expect it to..."

actualise quite like this. What woman would expect such a thing? I was hoping it wouldn't happen to you – to you and Jano. Last time you called, I thought you might be exaggerating a little. Because in our place it didn't grow quite so fast! Peťo and I had been together for six years by the time we first noticed it! But times have changed, the pace of life is accelerating... I know I'm probably not putting it well, but the fact is, the world's got faster, so that you and Jano... Even though you've only been together for two years – it has been two years, hasn't it? Or three? Anyway, for some reason it's happening faster. I'm being naïve, aren't I?"

"Soňa, I love you, you're my only friend. But why did you keep this of all things secret from me?"

"I'm telling you: I was hoping it wouldn't happen to you!"

"And what about your parents? At home, when you were growing up... Did they have a problem? You know what I mean."

"Of course. Nearly every family on our estate had it. I remember the Kropáčes, they had to move out because of it: it simply pushed them out of their flat. One morning it was sticking out into the hallway. Can you imagine how delicate the situation was? Real existing socialism, and there's something sticking out of the door of your flat? And you and your children are having to sleep on the stairs? Well, my parents took their children in for a few days, the kids stayed in my room, but I didn't like them, they cried all the time. By the way, it eventually turned out to be a blessing in disguise for the Kropáčes: it followed them everywhere; in the end they were staying in a workers' dormitory in Smíchov, in Prague, but one night, after it caused a scandal by swelling up, making the whole house burst, waking up half the city of a hundred spires, they took a radical step: emigration. Now they have a wonderful life in the West, she's living in Italy with the kids and he's somewhere in Switzerland. They split up as soon as they crossed the border. Don't you get it? It was a question of life and death. But actually, in cases like this, it's always a question of life and death."

"But why did my mum never even hint at it?"

"That's what women are like: though we can see – right from the beginning, actually – how things happen and how they're going to end, inevitably, we keep hoping... and making the same mistakes. We just don't learn our lesson. Most of the time. Not even seeing the way that our own parents have ended up prevents us from letting the same thing happen to us and our children. From their earliest days we push them to do the same thing to their offspring when the time comes. It's like some compulsion, can't you feel that?"

"Soňa! I thought I was going round the bend!"

"That's right. You are going round the bend, but nobody will notice you're mad. It's a collective madness. You're no different from anyone else. How do you diagnose madness if everyone is mad?"

Miša had no idea.

For weeks she just moped about the flat.

She could see it was watching her intently from behind the set. Or rather, not from behind but from underneath the TV, which by now was hovering above it, swaying from side to side like a vacationer on an air-mattress.

Miša stood on the balcony.

Miša leaned against the kitchen unit.

Miša even dreamt of going for a hike in the pure, unadulterated countryside.

And wherever she happened to be, she wondered what it was that she and Jano actually wanted from each other. Wherever she might be she also wondered how she could get into the wardrobe where she kept her large suitcase from before their marriage, because by now it was cluttering up the whole room, blocking the way to the wardrobe. And in the most extreme moments, between the thirteenth and fourteenth cigarette, between a wistful stare from the balcony down to the street and at the skyscraper opposite – into the windows of prison cells similar to her own – between times of calm resignation and quiet horror, in addition to other, more important and essential things, Miša also thought that you need a partner to do up the clasp on your necklace, and that you need a necklace to find a partner.

SPRING IS COMING

Who is this, the woman thought in the morning, gazing at her husband. She stepped back from the bedside table and went over to the wall without taking her eyes off the figure in the bed, then sighed and looked out of the window. She registered the dog in the large empty courtyard, another courtyard behind the first one and a house behind that, then another house and a hillock nearby.

Rolling countryside. Groves and vineyards.

Somewhere closer to the distant horizon the woman's eyes conjured up a forest and celestial birds flying high above it.

Who is this, she wondered later, in town on a Friday

afternoon. She peered out from behind a baguette shop. As she snooped on her husband she saw him walking towards the Montreal Pub with a couple of shabby individuals, slowly, swinging a briefcase that had once looked smart, happy about the fact that the weekend was about to begin.

She followed them inside.

"Ďusko, what will you have?" said a short guy.

"I've had a couple of gins already, so I wouldn't say no to another gin."

Who is this, she couldn't stop musing.

She leaned against the wall, half closing her eyes.

When she opened her eyes again they were gone.

She rushed to the station, hurriedly bought a train ticket, and having got off at her home station she slipped into Hilárik's, the dive at the end of the village. Catching her breath, she watched her husband, his head slumped over a shot of some translucent liquid, and wondered: who is this?

Who is this, she contemplated seriously the next day in the vineyard, observing through the gnarled vine stumps the carefree, roundish, badly shaven, ruddy face of her husband, muttering something as he fingered the plants with tired, solemn movements that seemed serenely slow.

The woman entered the empty house and started walking from room to room. She picked up a book by Seyfullina and read: "The earth, waiting to be fertilized, was breathing with an eternal longing for spring. People and cattle, every living creature, observed a primary law of life: the reason we were born, the reason we are alive, is to keep procreating." So this was how you were supposed to understand the meaning of life. As if she didn't know that! She, too, had procreated, but the children had grown up and long ago pushed off God knows where. She glanced at the cabinet, then past the cabinet and the kitchen cupboards through the door towards the hallway, past the wallpaper in the hallway, the coat hanger and the little cabinet full of junk, and out of the entrance door, at her husband, and the question popped into her head: who is this?

Who is this, she kept burbling to herself every day, first thing in the morning, before leaving for her badly paid job, whenever she caught sight of her husband's thin pale legs with their swollen ankles sticking out from under the duvet. They invariably reminded her of the extremities of an albino spider. Had she married an insect? Why did she do that? Somebody must have forced her! It was they who had made her do it! She pressed her lips together and clenched her jaws, full of anger and bitterness. It's all their fault! She glared in the direction of the village. Not really.

It's not just their fault.

She turned round and was horrified to see a mirror emerging from a dark corner. Behind it there was another mirror, reflecting what was reflected before it. And behind it there was a third, reflecting nothing. This mirror looked as if it had been printed in large capital letters, as a definitive answer to her question, but it was an answer she could not accept. Every other object cowered by her feet, tiny italics full of typos, omissions and factual errors. The sofa, covered in tattered pigskin, had been made this way. The conference table, its glass covered in fingerprints, had been made this way. The fingerprints screamed of another past, more affluent and meaningful, when young state officials, her husband's colleagues, used to gather round this table, wearing their status like ill-fitting, humiliating overalls.

From the hallway she could see that something was wringing the dog. Whatever it was, it first made the dog bark for a while, only to let it fall again, leaving it lying in front of its kennel. But suddenly it came back, whatever it was, and started hurling the dog around the courtyard.

Howling, muffled whining.

Sorrowful, stepped-on-the-neck, horrible-funny living noises.

She withdrew behind the curtain.

But after a while she inched forward again. Did the curtain just brush against her pointy nose or did it also touch her dry lower lip?

Whatever it was, it was dragging the dog behind the kennel, getting its body entangled in the chain and reducing its options. Soon there wouldn't be any chain left to yank its four spindly legs.

Somewhere in the wall a pipe started humming.

What does God look like just now, while He's doing all this, she wondered. Is He tall or short, He who is the archetype of everything? He is the one dragging the dog around the courtyard, and just now He felt like wiping the kennel wall with it. She sees it all because she's back with her nose in the curtain: the dog's fur is polishing the wood, forwards, backwards, forwards, backwards, is God fat or thin, is He the one who makes the dog raise its head and make its eyes stare at the door because the handle has moved: does God have a penis or does he not? The woman peeled herself off the curtain edging her way towards the entrance door: does God have a vagina?

The dog turned into a clump of pulsating tendons, tensing and relaxing and she sensed that all this was connected to her. It affected her intensely and directly. She was naked underneath it all. Who was doing all this? Who was this?

The blood-caked hairs on the dog's tortured body were turning into symbols. With a pained sneer she realised what they meant. She ran towards the dog, brushing through its hair roughly to stop the symbols spotting her, spelling her and articulating her as an incantation.

Then she decided to take a radical step. She went back indoors and with all the concentration she could muster dared to look straight into the mirror, deep into all the mirrors. Who was this, she felt like asking again. She kept asking the question, compulsively, over and over again. She looked straight ahead, finally whispering:

"Nobody."

She joined her husband in the kitchen. He was eating something, hunched over the table, every now and then turning the page of a newspaper. She said to him:

"You are..."

"What is it?" he said, startled.

"You are..." she hesitated.

"Yes?"

"You are mine and I am yours."

Afterwards Ďusko wondered if it was some uncertainty or fear quite unknown and alien to him that had made his wife's voice tremble, or was she just cold, as he had accidentally forgotten to turn up the heating that morning. But why should he have bothered? Spring was coming.

CONTAGION

One day, when I began to feel troubled by the furniture in the old house I inherited from my parents, I asked some people to help me clear out all the rooms, load the furniture onto a lorry and drive it to the outskirts of the city where we tossed all the rubbish into a ditch and covered it with big sheets of fabric. Back at home I treated my helpers to several bottles of delicious, robust wine and before long everyone was singing at the tops of their voices and staggering around the house... As their voices echoed about the place I was suddenly filled with dread at the prospect of spending the night alone in the house after everyone had gone. The immense silence was sure to have a devastating effect on me, I realised, as I paced to and fro fearfully, my eyes darting around like those of a small animal, looking for any sign of understanding in the increasingly clouded, unsympathetic eyes of these people. My helpers were rolling around the rugs on the floor, singing raucously.

And then a stroke of luck: a friend, who was passing by, looked in through the window. I asked him to come in at once and stay the night as the others were about to leave and it was now dark outside.

They left but hung around in front of the house for a good while, hooting with laughter and shouting loudly; some of them even tried to dance but gradually, one by one, they turned up their coat collars against the cold, and disappeared around the corner, even if their steps were slow and unsteady.

I offered my friend a slice of buttered bread with onions. He sat on a rug chewing intently: first one cheek bulging out, then the other and he licked a finger from time to time. His dark eyes gleamed in the light of the bare bulb. His thin lips, pressed together, resembled a scar from some appalling wound inflicted by a knife or a razor.

Ours was a weird friendship. In fact, we hated each other, but come to think of it, is it really so strange for friends to hate each other? We knew each other very well, having been friends for many years: time had turned everything that had been good and useful about our friendship incredibly dull and boring, depriving it of any value or else turning it into its opposite, until eventually all we did was watch out for each other's mistakes and blunders as an excuse for an argument. Even worse, there was an odd quality to our arguments, disguised as they were by smiles, magnanimous gestures and feigned understanding, and embellished with cunning compromises, behind which there lurked the next assault, to be launched cautiously and circumspectly, by innuendo rather than by direct accusation, of course, to prevent the adversary from mounting an effective defence, as he could never be sure just how and why he had come under attack.

My friend swallowed mouthfuls of the buttered bread, apparently expecting a night full of discussions of the kind where you have to weigh your words damn well, or, at least, as carefully as if making a move in a chess game with a grandmaster. But I kept quiet, leaning back against the wall. A growing sense of horror began to grip me. Responding to my friend's unspoken question about the removal of the furniture I blurted out that it had begun to trouble me of late, adding that what really troubled me was myself, the part of me which, through my long-term presence in this house, had invaded the old, cosy and otherwise quite blameless pieces of furniture. My words made my friend jump immediately to the conclusion that he possessed much greater, and rather more valuable, experience in this field. He compared the mystery of my furniture to that of Gothic cathedrals. I didn't really understand this comparison and it struck me as ridiculous. I lost track of the rest of my friend's explanation and couldn't wait for him to finish so that I could announce that now the rugs, too, had suddenly begun to trouble me, and I didn't hesitate to ask him to help me carry them into the back yard.

It was a chilly night but we didn't feel the cold; quite the opposite, we got rather hot and sweaty as we lugged the heavy rugs, some of which were really very large. Now and then we couldn't help swearing, especially when our load jammed in the narrow doorway and we couldn't get it in or out, clumsily twisting and yanking it through the entrance door. When all the rugs were finally in the yard I realised it wasn't enough: they still felt too close. My friend concurred, which I found surprising and encouraging at the same time, although I was also somewhat disconcerted by the potential hidden meaning of his unexpected agreement. So we discussed the matter for a while, yet I could not discern any evil intent on his part, nor any sign of a trap being laid, for my friend now confessed to having got rid of his own furniture and rugs some time ago, only he had been too embarrassed to tell me, assuming I would mock him for being a histrionic poseur. I readily admitted that his concern had been justified. Then we took the rugs and set about carrying them into a nearby grove where we piled them up and camouflaged them with branches, twigs, soil and stones.

Having returned to the house we lay down next to a wall, snuggling up to each other to keep warm, sipping the wine left over from earlier.

Then we slept until dawn.

A few weeks went by. My friend moved in with me, which naturally started the rumour mill in the neighbourhood; the women in our street were particularly outraged and some of them would cross over to the other side of the street rather than run into me on the pavement, while others even turned around and walked in the opposite direction. Far from being bothered by the reaction of the outside world we found it inspiring and bragged to each other about our burgeoning "negative" experiences.

People who had known us casually and learned we were now living together must have become suspicious about our sex lives although, in fact, any suspicion of this kind was absurdly misplaced: at first we even continued our relationships with our respective lovers and life went on as before until, eventually, we ceased to meet our lovers' expectations or, to be more precise, were no longer capable of satisfying their sexual demands – not necessarily because these had increased but rather because our potency had rapidly diminished until it virtually disappeared altogether; this change, however, was not the result of having relations with each other, as this never occurred, and in actual fact these – admittedly rather unpleasant – changes were the result of increasing exhaustion. This came about because after a few days of cohabitation we had both, quite spontaneously, reached the conclusion that we now felt troubled by the wallpaper and the wall-paint, as well as the parquet flooring and the lino; indeed, even the stone floor of the entrance hall and corridor had begun to affect us in the same way. And so every night after work we felt compelled to launch into gruelling physical labour in an attempt to purge our dwelling of the above-mentioned shortcomings. We would toil late into the night, and the entire house filled with dust and dirt; we would lie down to rest around midnight, only to be back on our feet an hour later and continue slaving away to ensure the house should feel like a genuine home. We spared no effort. We would load all the stuff stripped off the walls and taken up from the floor onto a wheelbarrow and bury it in the forest. This way of life so thoroughly drained us of energy that the thought of sexual gratification never even crossed our minds. Yet many people couldn't get our 'bedroom' mystery out of their heads, especially when they saw our haggard, exhausted faces, the bags under our eyes, and our emaciated bodies; on noticing our calloused hands the more malicious among them fantasized that we were engaging in some incredibly strenuous and perverted sexual practices.

Weeks and months went by. We bought new furniture and rugs. A short while later we had a removals company take the furniture away as it had started to trouble us inordinately, eating us up from the inside, and we began to perceive its presence in the house as some kind of saboteur or intruder who assaulted us with our own weapons, that is to say, our own character traits, which we had passed on to these objects, making them come to life.

Before long it was the turn of the rugs, those scheming serpents coiling around our feet and whispering to each other at night. We dragged them out into the yard and set them alight. Even as we looked into the flames we remained concerned that we might never be completely purged of this terrible contagion.

Soon we bought new rugs and new furniture. The furniture was modern and stylish and, later on, as we hauled it all to the dump behind the city, a large crowd of citizens gathered around with handcarts and barrows to snatch up the odd piece. We didn't care. We then rushed home for the rugs, rolled them up hurriedly, piled them onto the lorry and returned to the dump where people literally snatched them out of our hands, loaded them onto various means of transport and left, laughing happily; they thought we were crazy but, of course, fearing we might change our minds, no one ever asked why we were doing all this. For us it was no laughing matter. We began to wonder if our behaviour might be pathological. At this time we often wept, usually over a glass of wine, as we lay on the floor of the empty house; then we would again explode into bursts of almost feverish activity, scraping further and further layers off the walls, as by now they, too, had been contaminated with our presence and our existence. Every now and then we would reinforce the walls again and give them a new lick of paint, applying similar treatment to the floor but, nevertheless, the fits of destructive stripping of layers that we had contaminated were growing increasingly intense and frequent, preventing us from renovating our dwelling at a corresponding rate.

But there was worse to come.

What soon became even more unpleasant was the gap that opened up between how my friend and I perceived the process of contamination of our immediate environment. To cut a long story short, there came a point when the contagion engulfing the furniture and the walls began to affect my friend much more rapidly and with greater intensity than it affected me, his fresh fits manifesting themselves almost as soon as, say, new furniture had been delivered, the walls repainted or the floor replaced. One morning he came up to me and with a bear hug firmly declared that he was leaving since he could no longer live in the contaminated apartment. He went off to China and even though I have never heard from him since, my own predicament offers a clue as to his fate. Following his departure I threw out the furniture a few more times but eventually I stopped actively fitting the place out and continued to live in a house that was completely bare. It was, however, a terrible life. I was constantly haunted by an array of visions and hallucinations, my sleep disturbed by shadows that kept crawling from the walls towards me, shadows that resembled me to such a degree that I sometimes felt it was really my own self emerging from the plaster while the thing lying in the middle of the room on a pile of old rags was just a delusion that was bound to dissipate any moment. I could clearly see all my bad qualities emanating from the floor, peeling off from the wall paint, solidifying, and beginning to permeate me as they returned to their source. The severely contaminated house made the evil inside me expand continuously. I would strip the wallpaper off the walls with my bare hands, hack at the floor with a pickaxe, and rush to the forest carrying the debris in my arms, no longer bothering even to bury it. Soon the walls of the house were paper-thin. It did not take long for the first holes to appear and they grew bigger by the day. Eventually some of the walls caved in. The contagion grew daily more intense. I hired builders whose sole job was to dispose of the debris in the forest, covering it up with soil. I no longer had the time or energy to keep repairing and refurbishing the house. In the end I had mechanical diggers tear down the remaining walls, digging deep trenches where the foundations had been; these were filled in with lead. The plot was now unusable. During this period I lived in a tent, a new one every night; each morning the builders would drag it into the forest and destroy it.

I realised I couldn't possibly stay at home any longer. Only now did I reach the point my friend must have arrived at long ago. Now I understood how he had felt… The visions emanating from the contaminated objects, from the walls, the furniture – indeed, probably also from myself – must have had a horrifying impact on him! The sight of his own emanation from me would have presented him with an insurmountable, deadly problem, for while objects could be disposed of in one way or another, the evil in his own shape, emanating from me, threatened to endure forever… And even if I had vanished, the contagion had by now begun to spread from my friend at such a pace that it was almost physically impossible to keep up with it, to replace the furniture, renovate the walls, repair the flooring, and so on. He had only one option left, the same one I was facing now: to leave. What lay ahead for me now was a life on the road, in permanent flight. I left my native city. This wasn't too hard as I was no longer emotionally attached to it: I wasn't close to anyone since nobody would acknowledge me, my former friends pretended not to know me, the women I had loved had no use for an impotent, exhausted lunatic; my colleagues had signed a petition demanding I be fired claiming that I had a drink problem – and who wouldn't, in my shoes? But I'm not complaining. In any case, staying was out of the question. The contamination of my environment with my character traits was accelerating at breakneck speed: I couldn't stay anywhere for more than half an hour before my surroundings started to feel literally toxic, permeated by everything I represented and was most terrified of… It felt like being forced to look into a mirror all the time and being made to confront the worst aspects of myself… Even going for a beer was no longer safe because after about a half hour or so I felt a terrible compulsion to scrape off the plaster from the wall nearest to my table to stop seeing myself in it; a little later I started to wonder if it wasn't the person holding the glass that I should be digging my fingernails into because the figures on the walls and in the furniture seemed more real, more plausible, more alive.

I hit the road. It wasn't a comfortable life but I had no choice. At first I would spend the nights at railway stations and in barns, but later I found it impossible to rest, since after a few minutes an unspeakable sound, a chorus of whispering phantoms would rouse me from my sleep and I would find myself surrounded by multitudes of exact copies of myself and couldn't stay there any longer, not even for a moment, and felt compelled to press my hands to my ears and stagger out into the night.

Later I was no longer able to take just one step at a time and felt a compulsion to run, as my surroundings were now being contaminated by me at a dizzying speed. Once, as I was running, I saw a totally exhausted man collapse into a ditch by the road; he was obviously at the end of his tether. Running past him I noticed he was being inexorably deformed by some pressure whose source was invisible to my eyes although clearly discernible to him, as the expression on his face and his horror-struck eyes made clear...and within a few seconds he vanished, crushed by pressures that bore down on him from every direction. The poor man was simply sucked into the void. I moved on from the point where he disappeared and ever since have done nothing but trudge, trudge along the dusty road, fleeing a similar fate, although my strength is beginning to fail me.

This morning I crossed the state border.

AFTERWORD

The Carefully Disguised Meaning of the Text

*"Even people who love one another can drive each
other crazy sometimes."*

In the 1990s, when Balla first appeared on the Slovak
literary scene, stylized and playful writing, spoof and
pastiche was the dominant idiom among the emerging
generation of authors, partly in reaction to the socialist
realist prose favoured by their predecessors. Following
the Velvet Revolution of 1989 the demands of the market
seemed to pull writers in one of two basic directions: either
adjust to readers' expectations and marketability or, by
contrast, ignore them at the peril of being pigeonholed as
elitist. Balla chose the latter option, and despite winning
Slovakia's most prestigious literary prize, the Anasoft
Litera, in 2012, for his novella *In the Name of the Father,* his

audience has remained limited to a small circle of initiates. Balla's writing might be described as postmodern since, like that of other Slovak authors such as Pavel Vilikovský, Pavel Hrúz, Dušan Mitana, Peter Macsovszky and Tomáš Horváth, it is fragmented and "parasitical" upon other writers' texts and determinedly self-referential. Balla generates a burgeoning maze of meanings, creating characters whose loneliness is primarily a result of their otherness, whether intellectual or physical.

Balla's writing deconstructs everything his characters have endured, agonized over and suffered through and yet, despite its manifest stylization, their despair is credible, perhaps because they have sufficient reasons to feel sad. Balla's work articulates not only the isolation of an individual in the group but also the twofold loneliness in the relationships between men and women (*Zweisamkeit*, a story from his first collection *Leptokaria*, 1996, is a notable example). But faith brings no relief for his egodeistic protagonists either, as their relationship with God is highly problematic. Balla experiments with intertextuality, for example in *Tekuté poviedky* [*Liquid Stories*] in his 2003 collection *Unglik*, which "copy" works by Burroughs, Bukowski, Dostoevsky, as well as the Bible. Balla uses a method similar to Burroughs' in his *Nova Express*, except that the American writer's "fold-in" technique involves also quoting from his own fiction and journalism. Although Balla's references a number of authors and philosophers (Borges, Márquez, Derrida, Heidegger and Hegel, among others), particularly in his emphasis on existential anxiety, his style is very much his own. The author that Balla's bizarre portrayal of a dysfunctional family with a difficult, despotic father brings to mind most closely is Kafka, although Balla's postmodern treatment takes it to a new, extreme level. On the other hand, as Balla has said in an interview, he feels a certain affinity with Beckettian characters who have found themselves "in at the dead ends of existence", as well as with the work of Thomas Bernhard.

Balla's fiction is racked by doubt and often more is said between the lines. It is no accident that the protagonist of *In the Name of the Father* asks: "But why am I talking about my father?" The question is itself the answer. Fatherhood, parenthood, sonhood, partnerhood; these are the key themes of this novella, even if the narrator arrives at them by way of negation or subversion. The narrator – just like the protagonist of an early story, *The Hermit*, who asks "What would I do with a family?" – questions the purpose of the family; indeed, the doctor, a minor character in *In the Name of the Father*, advises the protagonist at the beginning of the novella that he should not procreate lest he bring more predators into this world.

So what is the world according to Balla like?

A character in another of his early stories, an elderly rubbish-dump guard who happens to be named Balla, has just completed a thousand-page long book "about life" which physically incorporates mirrors for increased verisimilitude. The mirrors reflect not only the mess and rubbish visible all around, but also things we neither want nor need: the dump functions as a postmodern metaphor for a specific type of writing that recycles earlier texts, while also highlighting those on the margins and minorities. Apart from the "waste" of the reality of the dump (and the world), a postmodern author who enters the realm on the other side of the mirror will discover further, especially textual, realities. Another character in the same story owns a copy of Lyotard's *La condition postmoderne*, yet reads the work of Vladimír Mináč, a quintessentially socialist Slovak writer. The narrator escapes from a life of "evil" into textuality, where the focus on the base and the ugly is complemented by reflections on the nature of narration, story, reading and words. Balla's works constantly stress the illusory nature of reality (text as a shadow of reality), of the literary work (text as a shadow of others' ideas), as well as of relationships (love as something alluded to rather than lived).

In spite of the unmistakable religious reference in the novella's title, *In the Name of the Father* debunks traditional values such as God, nation and family. We might say that the author holds nothing sacred except that it would be a truism for, unlike the surrealists, Balla is not bent on destruction. He "merely" doesn't want to lie to us that his characters live a life of luxury when in fact they inhabit a shack and subsist on bean soup, that they love one another when in fact the father prefers his horse to his son, and the son, in turn, wishes he could drown his father in manure, when a wife wields total power over her sick husband and the daughter-in-law hates her father-in-law because she believes he has ogled her lasciviously. Things aren't any better outside the protagonist's immediate family: a neighbour chases after his children with an axe, "clans of alcoholic workers and peasants, or oafs" hang around pubs, offering little evidence of a turtle-dove-like nation or of any ideals anywhere.

Balla is an author who views reality from an ironic distance, exposing repulsive physiological detail (bad breath, obesity, nose-picking, flabby thighs, hairy armpits, deformed bodies) as much as dysfunctional relationships. He presents the world as disgusting, chaotic and alienating by deploying the motifs of blood, death, pus, illness, cramps, nothingness, contagion, disintegrating bodies, houses being demolished or scraped clean. Balla's texts are populated by outsiders, pseudo-intellectuals, masturbators, schizophrenics, ironic feminists, "a moronic writer", a half-Gypsy woman, aggressive Amazons, beasts, monsters and ghouls. His interiors and exteriors are equally dismal: the walls are mouldy or bare, ceilings low, curtains grubby, the parks are run-down and the houses gloomy, plaster is peeling and walls are contaminated, a strange tree grows in the basement (and would that the tree were the only cause of the family's breakdown!), rooms reek of mothballs, black pigs wallow in puddles... In *In the Name of the Father* the protagonist's brother builds a house which, rather than being a love nest, turns into a peculiar maze with direct current instead of normal electricity, a place where one cannot live, only eke out an existence, and from which there is no escape. No upward motion is possible, characters who climb the stairs or go up in a lift usually come tumbling down, or live surrounded by heaps of rubble, the city shrinks or swells catastrophically. Evil cannot be stopped because it is often non-specific and socially unidentifiable (like the menacing "it" of *Before the Breakup,* the slimy substance in the basement of *In the Name of the Father*, or the spreading contagion in the story of the same name), and thus integral to the characters themselves. There is no escape from the imaginary contagion, even if one knocks down a house or crosses the state border.

Balla's narrator therefore cannot speak of "beautiful things" since he simply doesn't see any such around him. "Disaster should be expressed in a language that is itself a disaster", reflects the narrator of Balla's second collection, *Outsideria* (1997). While writers in the past presented an idealized version of reality, Balla doesn't smooth anything out, which is why his speech turns into a scattering of words, a grotesque babble. His protagonists are often misunderstood by others, there is no meaningful dialogue. Instead of communication there are pauses, noise, silence, only the text provides the narrator with some refuge, albeit temporary.

"The meaning will be carefully disguised", states the

narrator's brother in *In the Name of the Father*, as he builds what he claims is a house without frills. Balla's books also attest to something greater than his critical and nihilistic prose might suggest. We shouldn't rejoice, our existence has no meaning, Balla's protagonists assert. But, in a roundabout way, their author's writing implies that it ought to have at least *some* meaning...

MARTA SOUČKOVÁ
Bratislava, September 2016

Also available from Jantar Publishing

BLISS WAS IT IN BOHEMIA
by Michal Viewegh

Translation by David Short
Foreword by Veronika Pehe

A wildly comic story about the fate of a Czech
family from the 1960s onwards. At turns humorous,
ironic and sentimental, an engaging portrait of their
attempts to flee from history (meaning the 1968 Soviet
invasion of Czechoslovakia) – or at least to ignore it
as long as possible... Light-hearted and sophisticated
at once, this is a book that reminds us that comedy
can tackle large historical subjects successfully.

BURYING THE SEASON
by Antonín Bajaja

Translation by David Short
Foreword by Rajendra Chitnis

An affectionate, multi-layered account of small town
life in central Europe beginning in the early 1930s and
ending in the 21st Century. Adapting scenes from Fellini's
Amarcord, Bajaja's meandering narrative weaves humour,
tragedy and historical events into a series of compelling
nostalgic anecdotes.

www.jantarpublishing.com

Also available from Jantar Publishing

THREE FACES OF AN ANGEL
by Jiří Pehe

Translation by Gerald Turner
Foreword by Dr Marketa Goetz-Stankiewicz, FRSC

Three Faces of an Angel is a novel about the twentieth
century that begins when time was linear and ended when
the notion of progress was less well defined. The Brehmes'
story guides the reader through revolution, war, the
holocaust, and ultimately exile and return. A novel about
what man does to man and whether God intervenes.

KYTICE
CZECH & ENGLISH BILINGUAL EDITION
by Karel Jaromír Erben

Translation and Introduction by Susan Reynolds

Kytice was inspired by Erben's love of Slavonic myth and
the folklore surrounding such creatures as the Noonday
Witch and the Water Goblin. First published in 1853,
these poems, along with Mácha's *Máj* and Němcová's
Babička, are the best loved and most widely read 19th
century Czech classics. Published in the expanded 1861
version, the collection has moved generations of artists
and composers, including Dvořák, Smetana and Janáček.

www.jantarpublishing.com